A
Harlequin
Romance

OTHER
Harlequin Romances

by JANE DONNELLY

DARK PURSUER

by

JANE DONNELLY

Harlequin Books

TORONTO • LONDON • NEW YORK • AMSTERDAM • SYDNEY • WINNIPEG

Original hardcover edition published in 1976
by Mills & Boon Limited

ISBN 0-373-01993-9

Harlequin edition published August, 1976

Printed in Canada

CHAPTER ONE

ANGUS MCKENZIE, head of Publicity and Advertising Dept. in Lammas and Lammas, the huge four-storey store that dominated the centre of Moorton Fells, a Yorkshire town in the East Riding, put down the telephone and told Kate Howard, "Mr. Lammas wants to see you."

Kate was an attractive girl, tall and slender, her mouth full, wide and curving as though laughter came easer to her than tears. Her skin was translucently pale, and dark brown eyes and a mane of even darker hair made a striking contrast. Right now she was on her knees, painting a gnarled and eye-catching tree, black on white, that was designed for a backcloth to a display of raincoats in one of the windows.

"I'll phone him," she suggested.

"His secretary said to go and see him," growled Angus. "And don't be all day about it. There's work to do here."

"Sorry," said Kate, and laid down her brush.

This was a nuisance. Andrew Lammas was becoming a nuisance, and Kate was regretting the quirk of fate that had put her and her tray of coffee cups and doughnuts outside his office exactly a month today . . .

. . . She had been walking along the office-lined corridor, passing the executive suite, when the door of the general manager's office had opened and the general manager had come out.

Andrew Lammas was twenty-eight years old and handsome as an actor with his wide-set eyes and beautiful mouth and Kate, balancing her tray, had been ready to give him a good morning in passing, although he seemed so preoccupied that she was prepared for him to pass without acknowledging her. What she wasn't prepared for was that he should bump into her and send her tray flying.

5

It went with an almighty clatter, and Kate screeched and Andrew Lammas jumped. Her skirt was soaked with scalding coffee and she held it frantically away from her as he gasped, "Where did you come from?"

"Out of the woodwork," she snapped. "From the canteen, of course. Why can't you look where you're going?"

A couple of doors had opened at Kate's shriek and Andrew Lammas said to one woman, "Mrs. Yeomans, help this young lady, will you?" then he continued on his way down the corridor.

Mrs. Yeomans was quick and brisk as an executive secretary should be. She turned to a younger girl who was standing at the other door. "Clear this up, please, Daisy, and get some more from the canteen." She put a light hand on Kate's arm. "Come in here and we'll see what we can do for your skirt. You're not scalded, are you?"

Kate was not hurt, but she was hot with indignation; the least the man could have done was apologise.

"This is drip-dry," she said. "I'll wash it out," and she spent the next ten minutes in the cloakroom.

By the time she got back to her own department another tray of coffee and doughnuts had been delivered, and her colleagues were taking their coffee break.

Ken Reeves, who wore sandals and jeans and sloppy sweaters, was trying to grow a beard and had a crush on Kate, greeted her with, "Have you been knocking the bosses about?"

"He knocked the tray right out of my hand," said Kate. "He's a clumsy feller, isn't he?"

"Don't be hard on wee Andy," said Angus. "He can't help not being quite so clear where he's going as his brother is."

"I suppose I'm lucky it was Andrew who barged into me," Kate joked. "If it had been Connor I suppose he'd have walked right over me."

"Aye," said Angus. "If you were in the way that's what he'd have done."

They were fooling, of course, but everyone knew that it was Connor, the elder brother, who was in charge of the Lammas empire — two other stores like this, three hotels, warehouses, a private dock and a long distance transport company—and that nothing was allowed to stand in Connor Lammas's way. No one working for him minded that. If you were part of an organisation in these troubled times it was a comfort that the man at the top was a winner. Andrew was referred to in the store as our Mr. L., but Connor was *the* Mr. L., there were no two ways about that.

By afternoon the small accident of the morning had faded to the back of Kate's mind, when Andrew Lammas walked into the studio. Angus got up from his desk and went to meet him. This didn't happen often. Kate had never seen Andrew Lammas up here before—she had never seen Connor Lammas at all. Angus went down to conferences and when he was summoned, but it wasn't the head of department that Andrew Lammas was looking for now, it was Kate. He was telling Angus, "I've come to make my apologies to one of your staff. We barged into each other in the corridor this morning and my secretary tells me Miss Howard came off badly."

Better late than never, thought Kate; this is nice of him. She said, "Thank you, but there was no harm done."

"Good," he said, he was glad about that. He stayed a few minutes longer, looking at their work. Before he went he said to Kate, "Miss Howard, perhaps you'd have lunch with me tomorrow, I feel that I owe you—"

"You don't owe me a thing," said Kate cheerfully. "Your Mrs. Yeomans replaced the coffee and buns, so you don't have to take me out to lunch."

Andrew Lammas was taken aback. He hadn't expected breathless reaction, but he had expected her to accept. She

7

was a striking girl, completely unimpressed by the fact that he was a Lammas. She was smiling now. "Thanks all the same," she said dismissively, and because there were three men watching and listening he had to accept that and say good afternoon.

It was raining when six o'clock came round and Kate walked out into a miserable evening with her head down and her coat collar well up. She caught the bus to her shared flat in the suburbs round the corner, and as she hurried along towards the bus stop a car drew up just ahead of her. Andrew Lammas had opened the door and was asking, "Can I give you a lift?"

That was how it had started, a month ago. She'd asked him in for a coffee, and had to listen to the story of his life before Susan, one of her flatmates, arrived home from her job as a nurse at the local hospital. By then Kate was feeling it was high time for her guest to be going, and she saw him up the steps of their basement flat, into the hall, and out of the front door.

Susan was looking bemused when Kate got back. "Isn't he lovely?" said Susan, and Kate grinned.

"He is rather."

"You did say he was Andrew Lammas?" Kate nodded. "Wow," said Susan, "I bet you feel pleased with yourself."

"I feel rather sorry for him," said Kate.

"Sorry?" Susan yelped. "*Why?* Born with a silver spoon in his mouth."

"Not much comfort in that," said Kate, "if spoon and set belong to your brother."

That was Andrew's trouble, his brother was the giant, and Kate, who had finally agreed to have dinner with Andrew tomorrow evening, was less thrilled than she might have been. He was lovely to look at, but Kate didn't have too much time for self-pitying folk.

But Andrew Lammas had time for her. In the four weeks

that followed he had phoned her, he had come up to the studio. It was the talk of the store, of course, that most evenings he drove Kate Howard home, and most evenings they were together, often with Kate's friends.

So far as Kate was concerned he was a friend, like the rest, but he was finding her an exhilarating challenge. She wouldn't accept expensive gifts, she wasn't husband-hunting. When the subject of marriage had come up casually—a girl in Fashions was marrying a man in Soft Furnishings—Kate had said, "Good luck to them if that's what they want."

He was surprised at her tone. "Isn't it what you want?" and she had fluttered her long lashes and inquired sweetly, "Are you proposing to me?" Before he could answer she'd laughed, "Don't panic, and for goodness' sake don't propose, because I'm not a marrying girl. The idea of being tied to someone body and soul scares me to death!"

The fact that she was unattainable added to her fascination, the more he saw of her the more he wanted her. Yesterday he had sent her a dozen red roses, and last night he had looked at her in the candlelight of a restaurant table and asked huskily, "What would you say if I said I was falling in love with you?"

"I'd say it was the wine and the candlelight," she had replied, gaily but without coquetry, deciding there must be no more candlelit dinners for two, because there was no prospect of her ever falling in love with him.

And now Mrs. Yeomans was phoning through to say would Kate go down to Andrew's office.

"I'll be right back," she assured Angus.

Mrs. Yeomans' door was open and before Kate could tap on Andrew's door Mrs. Yeomans shot out and beckoned, "Come this way." She was whispering, and when Kate reached her she hardly made any sound at all, just shaped the name with her lips, her expression giving it all the emphasis it needed, "It's Connor."

9

Kate was surprised to feel her heart give a lurch, because what could Connor Lammas do to her, except sack her, and that wouldn't be the end of her world. Nothing at all, and yet she was scared for a moment. Mrs. Yeomans who, having seen the start of the 'romance', had felt involved all along, was rather excited.

She smiled at Kate as though they shared a secret, and opened the door from her room into Andrew's room, and said, "Miss Howard is here, sir."

All Kate saw or registered when she stepped across the thick carpet was the man behind the desk. He had Andrew's regular features, but his were heavier and stronger, with a lot more character. A bigger man in every sense. The shoulders were wide and powerful in the dark suit, and as he looked at her she thought—when they said you were tough they weren't fooling.

Almost certainly he stood over six foot, but he didn't stand. He said, "Sit down, please," but she stayed where she was, facing him directly across the desk.

"You sent for me," she said.

"You know why, of course."

She could hazard a shrewd guess and she said coolly, "Am I being vetted as a friend of your brother's?"

Of course she was, and he had disapproved of her on sight. He had grey eyes so far as she could tell. Andrew's were hazel, but Connor's looked like chipped ice. She raised her dark smooth brows as disdainfully as she could and stared right back at him.

"Miss Howard," he said, "I'm a busy man, so I suggest we dispense with preliminaries. You've been working in this store nearly seven months now. Going by your record—isn't it about time you moved on? I don't see much future for you here."

The bluntness of that took her breath away. As she gasped he said, "There would of course be compensation."

10

He was offering to pay her off and it was almost wildly funny. "With the obvious conditions," he said, "that you get away from here, and keep away from Andrew."

"You leave me speechless!" That was not quite true, but near enough. She was still gasping. "No wonder you're a tycoon—there can't be many about with your egomania. You really believe that because I'm just one of the staff I can't be good enough for a Lammas." She gave the name a derisive deference and Connor Lammas said crisply,

"This has nothing to do with your position here. This is a strictly personal assessment. You wouldn't be good for Andrew and in the long run I doubt if he'd be good for you."

He sounded as though he was chairing a selection board and she had applied for a post. There was a file at his elbow on the otherwise cleared desk. He turned a couple of the typewritten leaves, glancing down at them. "You're a restless young woman, aren't you? No roots, no family. You seem to have lead a nomadic existence, including, I see, some time living in an artists' commune in Wales."

She leaned forward, her eyes widening. He hadn't got this from Records, there were pages of it, and she squeaked incredulously, "You've had me *investigated*?"

He shrugged slightly as though it was the most natural thing in the world, and she had never been so affronted. Through clenched teeth she demanded, "What do you think I am?" and he replied calmly,

"Trouble, Miss Howard, that I intend to avoid. So—how much?"

She said almost silkily, "I think I'll stay around. Who knows, I might even help Andrew find enough courage to call his soul his own. Besides, I don't think you could meet my price."

There was little chance of Andrew ever asserting himself, he must be completely dominated by Connor for this charade to occur, but it was a good exit line, and as she turned to leave, her head held high, Connor Lammas said, "Miss Howard, you overrate yourself."

She daren't go back to work until she was calmer. She would break down as soon as she got among friends, and regret later that anyone had seen what Connor Lammas could reduce her to. She'd shed no tears because of him if she walked around town all day.

She got out of the store, and stayed out until she began to feel calmer. She was still seething, but at least there was no longer any danger of tears, although it was well over an hour before she went back into Publicity to face Angus's heavy sarcasm.

"It must be very nice to be the boss's friend and take time off whenever you feel like it."

"It wasn't Andrew who wanted to see me," said Kate, "it was Connor," and they knew from the set of her mouth and the flat tone of her voice that the interview had been painful. She went on with her work, pale but composed, and no one asked her what had happened.

Andrew phoned just before six o'clock. Kate happened to pick up the phone or she would have refused to go to it. As it was Andrew said, "I've got to talk to you," and she said, "No, thank you," and put it down again, and no one needed telling who that was.

Janice, the third girl in the flat-sharing trio, was in when Kate got home, frying sausages and trying not to drip henna rinse about. Her hair was plastered to her head and she was watching the clock for when her twenty minutes' colouring time would be up. "I'm going red," she announced.

"It should suit you," said Kate. Janice was a natural medium brown, and Kate dropped her handbag and her coat on the divan and stood with her hands on her hips looking at the vase of flowers. "I'll give you a dozen red roses to go with it," she said.

12

"You'll what?" said Janice.

"The red roses episode is over."

"Andrew? Oh no! What happened?"

"Connor happened."

"Connor Lammas? What did he do?"

"Had me investigated," said Kate, "and decided my background wasn't up to Lammas standards."

"What a cheek!" Janice was shocked and indignant, but relieved to see that Kate was smiling wryly so her heart was obviously not broken. Kate went into the kitchenette and turned the sausages and said,

"Goodness knows what was in that file, I've never done anything hair-raising. He didn't approve of me moving about, I suppose. And that time I was in Wales—he read that out as though it was one long orgy."

"The artists' commune?"

"Mmm. There were some funny characters there all right," Kate laughed, remembering, "but I was only there for about three weeks. I painted walls and a few pictures and I cooked, and that was about all I did do. Anything else was only in the mind of big brother."

She looked thoughtful and a little puzzled. "But you know, I don't think he judged me on that report. When I went in he took one look at me and that was it. He wouldn't have approved of me no matter what the report had said. When I asked him what he thought I was he said, 'I think you're trouble'."

Janice felt she could understand that. There was nothing meek about Kate, although she could be gentle. Kate had spirit, that made it fun to be her friend and share the flat with her, but if Connor Lammas had expected to see someone he could bully or frighten his first sight of Kate Howard might have come as a shock.

"I don't think I've ever wished trouble on anyone before," said Kate, "but oh, I'd like to trouble him, to shake him up.

Nothing vindictive, of course, just some little thing like pushing him off the top of Blackpool tower."

"You'd have to get him up the tower first," said Janice, and yelled, "My *hair*, I'll be overdone!" She rushed to stick her head under the tap, the water flowing orange into the sink, asking, "What has Andrew got to say about all this?"

"Nothing, I hope. I am through."

"You don't care, then?"

"Not nearly enough to take this kind of treatment," said Kate emphatically.

The three girls were eating their evening meal when the knock came on the door at the top of the stairs. It could have been anyone, but there was a strong possibility that it was Andrew and Janice hissed, "If it's him what will you do?"

"Send him home to Connor," said Kate grimly.

It was Andrew, handsome as ever, well dressed as ever, looking forlorn. "I have to talk to you," he pleaded.

"Talk to your brother," said Kate. "I don't want to listen."

"I can explain."

Her voice rose shrill and incredulous. "Explain why your brother had me investigated and then had the gall to try to pay me off?"

"It sounds awful." It certainly did. "But I *can* explain." She wouldn't let him through the door and he dropped his voice because down below Susan and Janice were straining to hear. "I wish I could make you understand. Kate, investigations are done all the time in business. Anyone joining any part of our organisation in any senior bracket gets checked out in all sorts of ways. The machinery's there. It's easy to set it in motion."

She didn't want to get angry again, but she could feel her cheeks burning. "What kind of excuse is that? Why did *the* Mr. L. decide that *I* should get the treatment?"

14

"Because I've made a fool of myself before," Andrew admitted, "and when I told my mother I was serious about you she was anxious."

"She need not have been," said Kate. Because Kate was not serious about Andrew, but he said eagerly now,

"I know that, but she isn't strong and Connor decided to check because she was worried, and he went too far."

"I rather thought so," said Kate. "Have you told him he went too far?"

He sidestepped that. "You wouldn't promise not to see me again."

"No," Kate agreed drily, "but that was because I wouldn't have put his mind at rest for my own oil well. I have no designs on you at all, Andrew, not a one."

Perhaps that was why he couldn't let her go now. She hadn't seen what he could do for her, the kind of life he could open up for her, and he pleaded, "Can't we be friends again? Please, Kate, will you come to my home on Saturday for dinner?"

She almost laughed. "You are joking? You don't think your brother would sit down at the same table as me?"

He took encouragement from her laughter and explained, "It's a dinner party. There'll be others. You're not scared of meeting Connor again, are you?"

She would rather not meet Connor again, because if she was honest with herself there was something about him that scared her. Something dangerous. Power allied with ruthlessness, probably. She said, "I'll think about it," and as she closed the door Andrew said,

"Thank you," although she had promised him nothing.

Susan and Janice were all for it. They wanted to hear what the inside of the fabulous house called Lammas Knowle was like, and who the other guests were, and perhaps a touch of drama when Kate met Connor Lammas again.

15

"You can't say no," Susan squealed. "You've got to go, Kate, even if you are finishing with Andrew. It'll give us something to talk about for weeks."

"Oh, that clinches it," said Kate. "I'll certainly go and stick my head into the lion's jaws for that!"

Andrew collected her on Saturday afternoon, and she was staying until Sunday morning. His mother knew she was coming, he had assured her, and his brother knew, and of course there would be no embarrassment for her, and she hardly admitted, even to herself, that her real reason for going was to show Connor Lammas he couldn't browbeat her. She would enjoy giving him a few worrying hours, while he wondered if she was still 'pursuing' Andrew.

She had been born in Moorton Fells and spent the first seventeen years of her life here, so she had seen Lammas Knowle from the road across the moors, but on this late summer afternoon the house looked fantastic. Built in grey stone, with turrets and towers, it had been an Elizabethan manor house called Knowle Castle, restored and partly rebuilt by a Lammas who bought it at the beginning of the nineteenth century and renamed it Lammas Knowle.

The five-mile drive from town across the moors was pleasant. They passed a few cars, no one on foot, the sun shone on bracken and ferns and sometimes, between the hills, the river glinted.

The manor house stood to the right of the road, about a third of the way up a hill, backed by a great horseshoe shape of crags. It was the same colour as the rock. Water flowed down the outside of the crags into a waterfall and lake on the west side. The stream from the east curved round to flow into the lake, and out from the lake into the river, so that the house was surrounded by water like a moated castle of old. A track from the road crossed a bridge, where it became very much private property, and Kate sat forward in the car, gasping like an impressionable tourist.

Andrew left the car at the front of the house and led her up a flight of stone steps to a huge black-studded door. While Kate was still staring around her the door opened and a man let them into a great hall, in which it seemed to Kate they could have fitted not only the house in which she lived but half the street. High above was a minstrels' gallery with so many doors that she wondered if even Andrew, who had been born here, could have said what was behind every one.

She was looking up at the minstrels' gallery when she heard the woman coming towards them across the hall. She had never met Mrs. Lammas before, but she recognised Andrew's mother at once. They had the same sweet smile and the same willowy build. Jennifer Lammas was still beautiful, but although she came towards them smiling she was looking anxious.

Andrew introduced them and Kate took the hand that was being offered her, and when Mrs. Lammas said, "You work with Andrew, don't you?" she agreed that she was employed at the Moorton Fells branch of Lammas and Lammas, and answered a few questions. Although if Mrs. Lammas had read that dossier Connor had acquired Kate couldn't be telling her much she didn't know.

She looked as if she knew the answers, while she went on smiling sweetly. "We're just having a few friends to dinner," she said. "You may know some of them."

Unlikely, thought Kate, and smiled too, then turned to see who was coming down the staircase as Mrs. Lammas and Andrew both glanced upwards.

It was Connor, in brown polo-necked sweater, brown hacking jacket, jodhpurs and riding boots, striding down the wide curved staircase, looking every inch the master of Lammas Knowle. All he needs is a couple of wolfhounds to call to heel, thought Kate sourly, annoyed at herself because she had glanced instinctively from Connor to the main

17

closed door, and had a moment of near-panic as though escape had been cut off. Escape from what? He could do nothing to her.

Andrew was saying, "Kate, you know my brother?"

"Oh yes." She hoped he wouldn't shake hands. It was stupid, but her hands were trembling a little, and she dug them deep into the pockets of her green corduroy jacket.

Connor was with them now. She hadn't seen him on his feet before, he hadn't stood to welcome her or to see her out at their last meeting. Now she saw that her guess had been correct, he was over six foot. He had been at ease and in command in that office with the trappings of ultra-modern commerce at his fingertips, and yet he was at home in this castle, built in almost barbaric days.

"How do you do?" he said. He didn't expect an answer, and if she had announced, 'I expect to drop dead in the next two minutes,' her reply would still have bored him. He looked through her and she drawled,

"I feel I should curtsey."

That brought the focus of his eyes on her and she wished she had left well alone, because they were dangerous eyes with a touch of both ice and steel. "Wouldn't that be rather out of character?" he said, and then as though he had spent as much time as he intended to spend on her, "See you all later," and he went out of the hall.

"Would you like to see the horses?" asked Andrew.

Kate would have liked to be shown her room, or anything that was in an opposite direction to the one Connor Lammas had just taken, but she could hardly say that, so she said, "Yes, please," and Andrew took her arm, and they followed Connor down flagstoned passages into a courtyard, and crossed towards the stables.

A jet black horse was being led out and it made a picture that caught Kate's breath. It stood about sixteen hands high, with a white star on the forehead, and a long mane and tail. It moved restlessly, tossing its head, and as they neared it it seemed to Kate that the dark brown eyes were flecked with gold.

Connor had vaulted into the saddle, and Andrew said, "That's Halla. He's half Arabian, bred in Co. Wicklow."

That didn't mean anything to Kate, except that here was a superb animal. She moved forward to stroke him and as Connor snapped, "Get her back," Andrew grabbed her arm again.

"Don't go too close, darling."

"Does he kick?"

"He might. Only Connor can ride him."

Connor reined and trotted out of the courtyard, through the archway, and Kate asked in a flash of perception, "You've never tried?"

"No, I haven't, but the last man who did ended up with a broken leg. Come and see my horse."

Andrew's horse was beautiful too, a chestnut, compact and sturdy, who was delighted to be petted, and took an apple from Kate and would probably have stood steady for her if she had taken up Andrew's offer of a ride. But she laughed and shook her head. "I can only ride a bicycle. I'd much rather walk round the gardens."

The gardens were almost wild, except for a kitchen garden which was carefully tended. The waterfall was beautiful, crystal clear water cascading down, and the lake had tiny waves ruffling its surface. There was a small island with a round stone building, and a wrought iron bridge reaching it in the middle of the lake, but they didn't cross, although Kate would have liked to have done.

She said, "That's a darling little house," and Andrew said,

"Damp as a ditch and cold enough to freeze you. Would you like to see the picture gallery, as you're so fond of paintings?"

"Very much," said Kate.

She had a marvellous time, looking at paintings in a long gallery that seemed to go on for ever. There was a superb collection ranging from old masters to modern works of art, and she said blissfully, "I could spend a lifetime just looking at these. You are so lucky to be living with them."

"Am I?" Andrew shrugged as though the masterpieces around bored him, and Kate said longingly,

"I'd rather stay up here than go down to a dinner party."

"So would I," said Andrew, slipping an arm around her, but she eluded him, asking about another painting, so that he followed her sulkily, answering briefly, until her shining eyes and her glow of sheer delight beguiled him out of his sulks.

By the time they reached the end of the gallery it was time for Kate to think about changing, and Andrew took her to the guest room where she would be sleeping tonight.

"Someone had better collect me," she said, "or I'll never find my way." She was serious about that. She would get lost in this labyrinth of passages and rooms, and Andrew smiled,

"I'll knock on your door just after seven."

"I'll be ready," she promised, and closed the door firmly.

This room was almost modern, even the four-poster bed with its prettily sprigged hangings and coverlet. Wardrobes and dressing table were fitted, and the carpet was rose pink, thick and warm underfoot. A small bathroom led off, and having looked around Kate opened the case and took out her dress.

The dress was long, with long sleeves and a high neck, in what looked like cream silk, and when her long dark hair was brushed and shining she hoped that she would be able to hold her own. In any case, she wasn't competing. She had come to dinner and her dinner was all she had come for.

She bathed, using the toiletries and remembering the brands to tell the girls, then she made up at the dressing table, got into her dress, and was brushing her hair with the silver-backed hairbrush, part of the matching set, when there was a tap on the door. She called "Come in" expecting Andrew, although it wasn't quite seven o'clock, but a girl stepped into the room and Kate turned on her stool and said, "Hello."

"Hello." The girl might have been a few years older than Kate. She was wearing a jade-green tunic dress and long jade earrings. She had large blue eyes, a small nose, and a rather babyish face, although she was looking at Kate now as though the big eyes didn't miss much. "So you're Andrew's little friend," she said.

"Not all that little," said Kate.

"No." The girl went on looking. "You're not quite what I expected." There was only one reply to that,

"What did you expect?" so Kate asked it and the girl gave an almost embarrassed grimace.

"Andrew hasn't been too selective with some of his girl-friends," she explained. "Up to now."

Up to now could mean that Kate looked like an exception, but whether it did or not Kate wasn't taking offence or getting into an argument about Andrew Lammas. She was the spectator this weekend. She said, "You seem to know who I am. Who are you?"

"Gail Gowerie." The name seemed familiar. "Supermarkets," said the girl. "And you're Kate Howard, aren't you?"

Kate must have been discussed and named, and she wondered if she should emphasise that although she was a friend of Andrew's she was in no way his personal girlfriend, but that might cause a flurry and Kate wanted to preserve the peace while she was here.

So she changed the subject and asked sweetly, "Is Connor selective in his girl-friends?" and Gail Gowerie almost choked.

"Connor?" She looked around as though he might appear out of thin air, and her voice squeaked, "Well, you know Connor."

"No, I don't," said Kate pleasantly, "but I'm sure he's selective."

"No one would dare play him up because he wouldn't stand for it," Gail went on. "He'd never get involved with anyone who was going to cause him any trouble," and at the second knock on the door she jumped quite guiltily.

"Come in," called Kate again, and it was Andrew this time, very Regency in a plum-coloured velvet suit and a frilled cravat. He glowered, seeing Gail, and demanded, "What are you doing here?"

"Saying hello to Kate," she said pertly. "Anything wrong with that?"

Kate was on her feet now, she would have walked out of the room with Gail, but Andrew's hand on her arm held her back until Gail was a little way ahead. Then he asked, "What has she been saying?"

"Hello," said Kate. "And that you weren't usually too selective about girls." Andrew scowled and Kate smiled to show there were no hard feelings. "She did say 'up to now', so perhaps she wasn't being bitchy."

"She was," muttered Andrew. "She's the girl my mother wants me to marry."

"She's very pretty," said Kate, wondering if Gail wanted that too. If she did it must be hard on her pride to be here tonight, meeting an apparent rival. Kate said, "Andrew, you and I are only friends. You do know that, don't you?"

"If you say so." But he still had her arm, and they came down the wide staircase entwined, which must have looked affectionate to those in the hall below.

Connor was there, dressed soberly in a dark grey suit. There were others, and the drawing room door was open and that was where they were heading, but as Andrew and

Kate came down the stairs everyone seemed to watch them, and Kate wondered what they had all been told about her.

She might have stumbled because she wasn't used to everyone staring at her, especially when she was negotiating a great flight of stairs in a dress that flapped round her ankles. She would probably have blushed to her hairline if Connor Lammas hadn't been looking up with open distaste, so that cold anger swamped her embarrassment. She was an invited guest, and if he lacked common courtesy she was hanged if she was going to blush for him!

She held her head high and smiled as Andrew said, "They're all old friends, you'll like them."

They all knew each other, they seemed very old friends, and when Kate was introduced they all smiled at her, their eyes probing while they made conventional comments. There were six other guests besides Kate, including one girl who never took her eyes off Connor, and all of them looked and sounded as though money had never been a problem in their lives.

This was the world of high finance, big business, private planes and yachts, villas in exotic places. Kate was out of her depth, of course she was, she didn't know the people they were talking about, she had never been near the places they were discussing. But it was as entertaining as a play to her. She watched and listened so that when she got back home she could mimic their talk and their gestures, describe the food and the clothes and the jewellery.

Mrs. Lammas was wearing a necklace of what were almost surely real and fabulous emeralds, which had to be an heirloom because a Georgian lady whose portrait hung in the long gallery had been painted in it. Fascinating, thought Kate. Lammas ladies have probably been wearing that for well over a hundred years, just as they have been sitting around this table on these chairs.

She didn't in the least mind being the outsider. She was

enjoying herself watching and listening. Connor talked least, but when he did he got everyone's attention. Everyone's but Kate's. She concentrated on her food, or played with her wineglass, or simply looked around her. She never once looked at him, because he could have spoiled the meal for her.

He didn't address one remark to her all evening. He ignored her as completely as she was ignoring him, and around eleven o'clock the guests began to leave. Kate was the only one staying the night and she wished now that she had asked Andrew to drive her back home; by staying here she could be putting herself in a false position, the party was over.

While Mrs. Lammas and Andrew were saying goodbyes somehow Kate was left with Connor, standing in the drawing room, with a glittering chandelier overhead, and no one else in the room. Before she could move he said, "I hope you've been entertained."

She couldn't leave the room now and she turned to face him, her own eyes narrowing as she met his eyes. "Immensely, thank you," she drawled.

He was smoking a cigar and he drew on it, then he said as coolly as though he was still talking to his after-dinner guests, "I should warn you that none of this will belong to Andrew, not even the emeralds my mother is wearing tonight. So if you're seeing yourself as the mistress of Lammas Knowle you can forget it."

She smiled, as seemingly cool as he, although her heart was racing and her nerves were tingling. "Now that doesn't surprise me in the least," she said. "You of course are the master of Lammas Knowle, and may I say how well you fit the part. All that's missing are a few wolfhounds for you to whistle to heel and you'd make a perfect medieval baron —in the days when the riff-raff had to ask leave to breathe. I suppose that horse of yours that nobody else is allowed to ride is the next best thing to a pack of wolfhounds."

He looked at her as though she was a babbling fool, and she lashed out, "The thing that would surely put any girl off Andrew would be the prospect of you as a brother-in-law!"

She shouldn't have said any of this. Now his eyes were hooded and his face was impassive and he spoke very quietly. "You show discernment there. Getting me for a brother-in-law would be the biggest mistake of your life."

Then he went out of the room, closing the door quietly behind him, and she was scared. She had reasoned that there was no way Connor Lammas could harm her, but every instinct told her now that in him she had a dangerous and implacable enemy.

CHAPTER TWO

THE bed had been turned down in Kate's room and the curtains pulled close, and a bedside lamp burned with a soft pink glow. It was a lovely room and perhaps she could pretend she was staying in a hotel instead of Connor Lammas's house, then she might sleep peacefully till morning.

When she parted the curtains to look out the moonlight seemed bright as day, showing the courtyard below and the encircling crags rising high. The house was a fortress, and again she had that crazy feeling of wanting to escape. She was saving up for a little car, and if she had had her own transport she would have crept out of the house and got away, but a five-mile walk across the moors would have been a lunatic risk to take, the bed with the smooth sheets was soft and comfortable, and after a while she fell asleep.

She woke what seemed hours later, in darkness, and was stark awake in seconds. Something tiny and furry had scuttled across her foot under the bedclothes. A *mouse*. It must be a mouse. She dived out of bed, ending flat on the carpet, scrambling up and on to a chair, where she sat with her knees under her chin and her bare feet well off the ground.

She wasn't really scared of mice, but the thought of a mouse in the bedclothes was giving her teeth-chattering jitters, and it was a real effort to force herself to put her feet back on the carpet and get across to the wall switch.

Once the light was on her panic abated. It was always possible the mouse had run back into its hidey-hole, but she would strip that bed very carefully before she would risk it again, and then she would sleep with the light on and lie on top of the counterpane. Very gingerly she lifted the counterpane, ready to leap away the moment a mouse revealed itself.

It had to be a mouse. It couldn't have been a small rat. If it was a rat she wouldn't care who she woke, she'd scream her head off. She tugged at the sheets, gradually easing them off the bed, chewing on her lip apprehensively.

When she saw the mouse it was minute, with bright beady eyes fixed on her. There it sat, and after an instinctive shudder she couldn't be scared of it. She said "Shoo", but it didn't move. It was paralysed with fear, so she either had to leave it where it was or pick it up. She almost left it. Then she pulled herself together—for goodness' sake, it was tiny and terrified—and got a light soft scarf out of her case and gently scooped up her unwelcome visitor.

She ran a little way down the corridor and unwrapped him on the floor. She had done all she could for him and she hoped he would recover from his traumatic experience, although he had probably put paid to her night's sleep.

The corridor was dark as she walked back to her room, but right down the corridor an open door led into the picture gallery, and the moonlight in there was so bright that Kate could see a picture on the wall, looking strangely ghostly. She wondered which picture it was, and when she came to the door of her own room she passed by, going on along the corridor into the gallery.

It was a portrait of a small child in a dimity dress. Kate remembered it by daylight when the dress had been blue and the child had held a nosegay of pink flowers. It was a delightful painting, but the moonlight that drained it of colour gave it magic. The whole great gallery had a haunting quality and Kate walked in wonderment from picture to picture.

When she heard the footsteps she felt like a thief in the night. She was doing no harm, but it wouldn't be easy to explain what she was doing at this time, easier to beat a hasty retreat, and she would have done just that if she

27

hadn't recognised the man who had come into the gallery and was now walking towards her.

That froze her like the mouse. She couldn't run. She could only shrink back into the shadows and wait while Connor Lammas came through the pattern of light and shade that windows and wall threw on the polished floor. He was fully dressed, as she had seen him last, while she was barefoot in a white cotton nightdress and she wished that the ground would open and swallow her.

Of course he had seen her, right down the gallery, and he didn't believe in ghosts, because when he said, "What are you doing here?" it was the tone he used for Kate.

She gulped. "Looking—at the pictures."

He seemed even taller in this distorting light as he stood a couple of feet away from her. "In the dark?" His tone was ironic and she protested,

"There's moonlight."

He didn't argue. He said, "I'd prefer you to stay in your own room rather than prowl around. Unless of course you're on your way to someone else's room."

He meant Andrew's, he meant—oh, she longed to hit him right across the face, but somehow she kept her voice almost steady. "I couldn't care less whether you believe me or not," she said, "but there was a mouse in my bed, and I caught it and took it out into the corridor to let it go, then I saw the gallery in the moonlight, so I came to look at the pictures."

She didn't want to walk ahead of him. Her nightdress was all she was wearing and she wasn't sure how revealing it might be if she got herself silhouetted in the moonlight. Of course she had been stupid to wander around without even putting on a dressing gown, but she had expected everyone to be asleep hours ago. She said, "You prowl around quite often in dead of night, do you?"

"It's hardly midnight," he said. She had thought it was

28

much later, three or four in the morning, she had thought. "Goodnight," he said coldly.

She clutched her nightdress to her to provide the best possible coverage and backed away to cross the gallery quickly on a bridge of shade, and Connor Lammas said drily, "You're still overrating yourself, Miss Howard."

That was what he had said at their first meeting, "You overrate yourself." Now he sounded as though she thought she was so seductive in her cotton nightgown that she daren't step out of the shadows in case he should grab her.

She ignored that. What else could she do? She knew she was about as desirable to Connor Lammas as he was to her, but she was not in the habit of parading herself and she was embarrassed, caught like this. She walked quickly until she came to the painting opposite her corridor. Then she dived out of the gallery with the relief of a pickpocket dashing into an alley.

The girl in the dressing table mirror looked dishevelled, dark hair falling over her eyes, her face flushed and her breast heaving as though she had been fighting or running for her life, and Kate was quite shocked to see herself. Each time she had come up against Connor Lammas she had ended like this, feeling furious and helpless, and it was her own fault this time for coming here. She hadn't come because Andrew had asked her and the girls had urged her, she had come to show Connor Lammas that he couldn't dictate to her. No more could he, but he could scare her so that she was frantic to escape, and he could make her look like this.

Andrew must take her home right after breakfast, or she would walk, and she would never let this happen to her again. She turned from the mirror and remade the bed, then left on the light and slept on top of the counterpane. There was no sound or sight of any more mice and she fell asleep at last.

The girl who brought in a morning tray of tea looked curiously at Mr. Andrew's new girl-friend who slept on the bed, not in it, and Kate explained, "A mouse ran over my feet, under the sheets."

The girl wore no make-up and only just escaped being plain, her hair was pulled tightly back in an indiarubber band, raising her eyebrows and giving her a startled expression. Right now she was startled. "Oh dear," she said, "I'm ever so sorry. There are a couple of cats."

Kate smiled, "It was only a tiny mouse. I hope the cats don't get him."

The girl smiled back, "There's a lot of room for them to go."

"There certainly is," Kate agreed. "Could you show me where the family have breakfast?" The girl came back fifteen minutes after she had brought in the tea, and took Kate downstairs to a room where Mrs. Lammas was sitting all alone, looking as fragile as the thin china cup she held.

"Good morning," said Jennifer Lammas. "Do sit down. What will you have for breakfast?"

"Just tea and toast, please," said Kate. That was already on the table, with butter and honey and marmalade. The table was laid for four as though one place had been cleared, and Kate hoped that was Andrew's because if he was up she could get away soon. Then Mrs. Lammas said,

"Andrew isn't down yet. Milk and sugar?" and as Kate took the cup, "What are your plans for today, dear?"

Escape, thought Kate. She said, "I must be going soon. I have some work to do."

"Oh, what a pity, this has been a brief visit. Next time you must stay longer." Jennifer Lammas didn't mean that, it was what she usually said to departing guests, and Kate said quietly,

"Thank you." She could read Andrew's mother's thoughts, but Andrew's mother couldn't read hers, and Jennifer Lammas suddenly dropped her pretence that all was well and leaned forward with pleading eyes.

"Kate, there's something I think I should tell you." She sounded almost timid. "About Andrew. Don't get too fond of him, because he is rather impulsive in affairs of the heart. What he says today is often very different from what he feels next month, and I wouldn't like you to be hurt, and you might be and so might Andrew."

Kate said gently, "You don't need to worry, Mrs. Lammas, Andrew and I are friends—"

"Just good friends," said Connor sardonically. She hadn't heard the door open nor heard him come into the room, but now she felt his presence like a dark shadow across her, as he walked past the table and stood by the fireplace, facing her.

"That's right," she said, and she was not going into greater detail for Connor about her lack of feeling for Andrew. She pretended to drink some tea, and after a few moments' silence Mrs. Lammas said,

"Kate was just saying she has to get home."

"She is in demand," said Connor. Kate sat stoney-faced, ignoring him.

"Have you seen Andrew, dear?" asked his mother, again after a short silence.

"No," said Connor, "but if Miss Howard is in such a hurry I can run her back home myself."

Kate almost choked, her teacup at her lips, as she imagined being shut up in the cabin of a car with Connor Lammas for five moorland miles. "No, thank you," she gulped, "I'll wait for Andrew."

"I thought you would," he said cynically.

Mrs. Lammas looked from Kate to Connor, then she said, "I'll see what's happened to Andrew."

Kate poured herself more tea, although her cup was still half full, then she looked up again at Connor. If anyone broke the silence it would be him. If she spoke it would be something she would regret later, such as, "Stop looking at me as though you can't imagine what any man could see in me. Just *stop* looking at me!"

He went on looking at her, for less than half a minute, but time stopped until Kate almost screamed. Then he went out of the room without saying a word, and that was an insult. It made her nothing, invisible, and as soon as the door closed she jumped up.

She would have loved to smash something, hurl a cup against the wall or into the fireplace. Instead she paced up and down, working off tension in silent action, because he built up tension in her as no other man had ever done. And when Andrew came into the room the words that came from her spoke themselves. "I want to go home."

Her vehemence startled him. "What's all this about?" he wanted to know, and she knew she was being unreasonable, it wasn't Andrew's fault that Connor was intolerable.

"I'm sorry," she said. "But I must be on my way. I have some freelance work that has to be finished today. Please will you take me?"

"If you insist," said Andrew stiffly.

When they had driven across the bridge over the stream coming to Lammas Knowle yesterday Kate had leaned forward, thrilled at the sight of the magnificent old house. Now she looked at the house again as they came to the bridge, turning in her seat beside Andrew, holding her breath as though she had expected a pursuer and was only safe when the bridge was crossed.

Andrew, who had been silent and offended up to now, burst out, "You never said anything about freelance work before. Why are you rushing back? What went wrong? I thought you enjoyed yourself yesterday."

"I did." There were patches of her visit that she had enjoyed very much. She said. "But your mother's worried,

32

and you shouldn't be worrying her when there's no reason. You and I are going no further. We're friends of a sort, but no more."

"Why not?" The petulant note was in his voice, but she tried to be kind.

"Because—oh, you don't really want to get involved with me."

"I *do*." He sounded like a spoiled child, denied a toy, and she said, half smiling,

"Only because I don't want to get involved with you. Or with anyone else—this isn't personal."

"I do have money, Kate. It isn't all Connor's, you know, I'm pretty well heeled, I could give you anything you wanted."

She made no reply and he glanced sidewards at the clear cut cameo of her profile, and the raven dark wing of her hair, and asked, "What do you want?"

"Nothing that costs much," she said lightly. "Nothing I can't work for."

He carried her small case to the door of her house and she said, "Thank you, and goodbye for now."

"Do I see you tomorrow night?"

She hoped to make the break gradual and gentle, so she said, "Come to supper on Wednesday if you like," and Andrew accepted that with a bad grace and scowled as he got back into the car.

Janice and Susan hadn't expected her back so soon. Susan was still in the divan bed, talking to Janice, who was cooking breakfast. As the door opened at the top of the stairs Susan jerked upright and Janice came out of the kitchenette, pyjama-clad.

"What are you doing back?" Janice demanded. "It isn't ten o'clock yet. We thought you'd be staying for dinner again."

"I hardly got breakfast." Kate grimaced. "In fact it was

over breakfast, just the two of us, that Mrs. Lammas warned me that Andrew's offers of deathless devotion rarely last the month out."

Both girls were shocked, and Susan gasped, "What a beastly thing to say!"

"No," said Kate, dropping her bantering tone, "she was rather sweet. She didn't want anyone hurt—including me."

"What about Connor? How did you get on with him this time?" Janice asked, and Kate looked down her nose in a caricature of arrogance.

"Oh, he looked straight through me. So far as he was concerned I wasn't there." The girls giggled and she grimaced again, dismissing Connor. She could talk about everyone else and she gave them a hilarious account of her visit, including the mouse running over her toes in the middle of the night, but the name of Connor Lammas reached a deeper level where there was too much feeling. She couldn't trust herself to talk about him without betraying real hurt and anger.

"Andrew's coming to supper on Wednesday," she said, "and I'd appreciate it if you both hung around. I don't want a cosy twosome."

"What are you expecting," Janice asked, "a pass or a proposal?"

"I could deal with a pass, but a proposal would be embarrassing." ·

"You wouldn't marry him?" Both girls said more or less that. and Kate shook her head.

"It's quite out of the question." She picked up her case and went into her tiny little room to unpack, and Susan and Janice looked at each other.

"That was emphatic enough, she wouldn't marry him." Susan sounded wistful because Andrew Lammas was so handsome and so eligible. Kate had always said she had no plans for marriage. So did Susan and Janice sometimes, but they didn't mean it and it was beginning to look as though Kate did.

Susan whispered, "Did you see her shiver just now, and the look in her eyes as though she was remembering something? Did Kate ever have a love affair that went badly wrong?"

Janice had seen the bleakness in Kate's eyes and been shaken. She shook her head and whispered back, "If she did I never heard about it."

Kate wasn't unpacking yet. She had put down her case and she was sitting on her narrow bed, remembering. Her attitude towards marriage had been caused by a love affair that went sour. Not her own, her parents'. There must have been a kind of love between them at first. They were a physically attractive pair before self-pity thinned her mother's lips and blurred her father's features. To friends and neighbours they were an ordinary enough couple; he managed a hardware shop while she ran the home. They were highly respectable, but when they were alone, no one watching or listening but Kate, they lived in hell. There was no charity in that home, no support. They drained and denigrated each other in a hundred ways, her father blustering, her mother whining.

Kate came home from school almost daily to listen to her mother's complaints and to promise that she would never leave her. Her father was always threatening to walk out, but he never went, and he never would have gone. Man and wife clung to each other like a drowning couple, each blaming the other for dragging them down, until the day they died.

Until the moment they died. Kate was in the back seat of the car. An argument was going on in the front seat, and then the crash came, and later in hospital they had told her she was alone.

She had wept, of course, but slowly she had realised that

35

she was not so much alone as free. It was strange to find the world opening up around, to discover that her horizons could be limitless where she had once been confined to a house like a prison.

She was working in a newsagents just around the corner from her home; the house hadn't belonged to her parents, there was nothing to keep her here. She applied for a job as a waitress at a small seaside hotel, seasonal work. That winter she was a filing clerk for a while. She made friends wherever she went and she enjoyed life.

She kept in touch with old friends, too. Janice and Kate had gone to school together, but none of her friends ever suspected how miserable Kate's home life was. Even as a child Kate had had too much pride to talk about her troubles; she didn't want anyone feeling sorry for her. So that when, seven months ago, Janice wrote about the bed-sitter she was sharing with a super girl who was a nurse, and how about Kate coming and making a threesome, Janice had no idea how ironic it was to ask, "Don't you ever feel homesick for the old town?"

Homesickness for her childhood was something Kate would never know, but the idea of sharing the flat appealed to her. She had always liked Janice, and she and Susan took to each other on sight, and when Kate went through the local newspaper on her first night here, looking for a job, she found the vacancy in Publicity advertised.

Everything had worked out marvellously, perhaps too well. Kate had settled in with no urge at all to move on again, but Andrew Lammas could disrupt her orderly and satisfying existence. He was waiting for her next day when she came out of work and she said, "I can catch my bus quite easily."

"Not as easy as getting into the car," he said.

"I can't ask you into the flat and I do have a date this evening," she explained.

36

"Who with?"

The car park was crowded as it always was at this time, and those nearest were listening as they passed, but she said, "None of your business."

"All right," he said, "we won't discuss it. Come on." Accepting a lift was hardly committing herself for life, so she got into the car and Andrew turned on the radio and they didn't do much talking. But when the car stopped and Kate got out Andrew said, "I love you, Kate."

"I doubt that," she said, "and I'm not in love with you."

"We'll talk about it on Wednesday," he said as he closed the door and drove away, leaving Kate standing on the pavement with a sinking heart. It seemed that Andrew Lammas believed there was nothing he wanted that he couldn't have, and she might as well hand in her notice to Angus tomorrow, because as Connor Lammas had pointed out, there was no future for her at Lammas and Lammas.

Angus took her resignation regretfully and asked, "You're really set on going?"

"I'm sorry," said Kate. Angus sighed gustily, then he said,

"Well, if you've definitely made up your mind how would you be feeling about a job in an art gallery in London? Felix Klopper's well known in the art world, and so is his gallery, and when he was down here some time ago he saw some of your work." Kate's eyes widened; this was the first she had heard of this. "He was taken with it," Angus went on. "So much so that he told me he'd give you a job any time."

"But why didn't you tell me?" Kate wondered, and Angus said promptly,

"Because I didn't want to lose you, but if you're set on going I can't think of a better opening for you. Your job would be selling, but you'd have a chance to paint, and if you produced anything worth while it would be put in the

37

gallery and you'd be likely to get a very good price for it."

She would hate to be leaving the girls, but this sounded like a marvellous opportunity. Even if her work was never up to gallery standards she would be handling work that was, meeting artists and art lovers, spending her days among beautiful things.

Angus looked so serious that he sounded fierce: "I think you've got talent and you're wasting it here," he said. "You go and take your chance, lassie, and when you're famous we'll be proud to have known you."

He was teasing her, of course, but he made her smile, and suddenly it seemed that something good was coming out of this tangle.

When Andrew came to supper next evening he got a cool reception from Kate's flatmates, who both blamed him for causing Kate to leave town. Kate had charisma, she brightened everyday life, and living with her they had discovered a quality of steadfastness. They knew they could have relied on Kate and they were going to miss having her around the flat.

Kate had cooked a curry, which they all ate at the little table, making polite conversation. Then Susan washed up, and Janice turned on the television and sat in front of it, while Andrew and Kate sat on the divan. There were no signs that Janice and Susan were going out this evening, in fact Janice was saying, "I suppose I might as well wash my hair," and Andrew's chagrin was mounting.

Kate knew he had wanted to talk to her. She was curled up now, with her head resting almost sleepily on a cushion, and Andrew said, "I want to talk to you."

She looked at him with drowsy eyes. "No one's stopping you."

"No?" He indicated Susan and Janice. "Please," he said, appealing to them, and Janice offered,

"We could go upstairs and watch this on Mrs. Harris's

telly." Susan agreed eagerly,

"Yes, we could do that." Janice was feeling embarrassed, Susan believed in happy endings, and thought that Kate should listen to what Andrew had to say, and Kate was sorry she had drawn her friends into this awkward scene.

"All right," she said, and Andrew smiled gratefully at Susan and Janice as they went.

When the door at the top of the steps closed he turned to Kate and said abruptly, "If I asked you to marry me—"

"Please don't," Kate pleaded.

"Why not?" Having reached a proposal he could not envisage refusal. "My mother will come round, she only wants what I want, and once we're married Connor won't waste his time making a fuss about it."

At the mention of Connor's name Kate tensed, and Andrew went on eagerly, "He needn't know until we're married, we can get a special licence."

This was pathetic. Andrew would make his marriage a hole-and-corner elopement rather than risk Connor's wrath, until wrath could serve no purpose, when Connor would presumably make the best of a bad job. As proposals went this was an all-time low, and Kate couldn't imagine any girl with any pride being flattered by it, no matter how eligible in the material sense Andrew Lammas was.

She asked quietly, "What can you offer a girl, except a life overshadowed by your brother?" and Andrew reddened, touched on the quick, mumbling,

"What do you want me to do?"

"I don't know." She was exasperated at his lack of spirit. "But for your own sake stand up to him. Leave your job if it bores you and do some writing." He'd once said he wanted to write. "Ride that great horse of his to prove you're as good a rider as he is, you're certainly as good a man, so stop dancing to his tune in everything."

Andrew said nothing, and she said no more, and at last he

asked heavily, "Are you through?"

She was through, and sorry because he looked more miserable than she had ever seen him look. Knowing her hadn't done Andrew much good, and this really must be a final goodbye. She told him impulsively, "I'm going away."

He stared at her. "Where?"

"I'm getting a job in a London art gallery." She might as well tell him the rest, he could soon find out. "Felix Klopper's Galleries," she said. "He knows Angus and he saw some of my work and he said he'd give me a job."

Andrew laughed, the kind of laughter that meant she had been duped. "He knows Connor too," he said. "Connor owns half those galleries."

Her house of cards came tumbling down. So it had only been another kind of bribe to get her away. Her work hadn't really been admired, no one had really thought she had too much talent to stay in Publicity.

"What did you say about dancing to Connor's tune?" jeered Andrew. He stood up then and said, "Goodnight Kate, I'll think about what you said. You think about what I said."

She nodded, dumb with disappointment. She had been a fool not to suspect, and if the offer had come through anyone but Angus she might have done. But Angus was always so straight that even now she couldn't believe he was party to a plot.

Next morning, as soon as she got to work, she asked him, "When did Mr. Klopper suggest giving me a job?"

Angus's wrinkled face creased deeper, following the drift of her question. "Last Thursday," he admitted.

Kate had been prepared for his answer, at least it meant that Angus wasn't trying to fool her, and she demanded, "Didn't you think it was rather a coincidence, so soon after my interview with Connor?"

"Aye," said Angus.

"It was to get me away from here, wasn't it?"

Angus was sitting at his desk. He made a sweeping gesture as though he was clearing it, or the situation, of clutter, and growled, "I don't give a damn what it was for. It was a genuine offer, so why can't you take the job? You'd earn your salary, and you've got a talent that could grow if you gave it half a. chance." He was half bullying, half coaxing. "Don't be a fool to yourself, lassie, take your chance."

But Kate shook her head, slowly and reluctantly. "I can't," she said. "I wish I could, but not from Connor Lammas."

Andrew kept away that day and Kate did her work with her mind in turmoil. She would.be sorry to be leaving here, she had been very happy, and there were times she wondered if she was being over-hasty. Until she had bumped into him in the corridor she had rarely seen Andrew Lammas, so why couldn't it be like that again? Andrew wouldn't want to look ridiculous in front of his staff. If Kate told him, emphatically enough, to keep away from her surely he would.

When she left work that evening she was still undecided, although she believed she still had free choice, to stay or go. She had no idea that she had passed the point of no return and from here on she had no choice at all, except perhaps the small one, whether she should get into Andrew's car in the car park.

She had half expected him there, but before she could speak he said, "Not a word about marriage, I promise you. You were right."

If he was going to be reasonable her troubles were over. He opened the car door. "And about other things," he said, "I have let Connor overshadow me. From now on it's going to be different." She got into the car, listening to him. "Starting right now," he went on. "And I want you to see."

"Where are we going?" she asked.

"To my home."

That was what she'd thought, and she felt like someone who had lit a fuse and was now riding towards the explosion. "What exactly did you have in mind?" she asked, and Andrew turned on the car radio, loud.

"You'll see," he said.

From then on she could only get monosyllables out of him. He seemed nervous, keyed up, certainly in no state to face the ice-cold Connor, and when Kate had urged him to step out from Connor's shadow she hadn't meant a face-to-face with Andrew in this jittery condition.

Andrew could hardly be telling Connor they were getting married so long as Kate insisted they were not, but he might be telling Connor that he would stand for no more interference in his private life. He might say that he was in love with Kate, and then she would get the brunt of Connor's contempt, and if that happened she would tell the pair of them that she wouldn't take on a Lammas if he came with the crown jewels. Then she would say good luck to Andrew, and goodbye to both of them, and this time she *would* walk back.

This time Andrew drove under the archway into the courtyard at the back of Lammas Knowle. There were people moving around. Doors into the house were open, Mrs. Shale the housekeeper was talking to a man who looked like a gardener.

Andrew got out of the car leaving Kate to follow, and went towards Halla's stable. The top half of the stable door was open, Andrew opened the bottom half and went in and Kate heard raised voices, and suddenly it dawned on her exactly what was going to happen.

"It'd be more than m'job's worth," a man was protesting loudly. "The master'd have m'hide."

The voices carried. Mrs. Shale and the gardener moved across to the stable where Andrew was commanding in high-pitched tones, "Bring him out. He's saddled, isn't he? He's ready."

"He's saddled for t'master."

42

"He's saddled for me. I phoned through."

"He'll throw you. He won't let you ride him."

Inside the stable the groom held the bridle at the horse's head. Halla moved restlessly, sensing tension, jerking his head and treading the ground, and Kate cried, "Andrew, don't!"

He took no notice of her. He moved with an outstretched hand as though he would lead the horse out himself, and the groom said sharply, "Don't wave your hand in front of him. Stand back and I'll get him out, but you're not riding him till t'master's here."

It seemed to Kate that the horse's gold-flecked eyes were red-rimmed, and surely even a docile animal would be disturbed by the argument raging around him, with the groom hanging on to the bridle and Andrew clutching at the reins. Halla's strong neck arched, ears flat, nostrils dilating, and from the way he was sidestepping any moment those iron-clad hooves would be lashing out.

Andrew seized his first chance to put a foot in the stirrup and mount into the saddle, while the groom let fly a colourful stream of invective.

"Watch this, Kate," called Andrew, turning Halla's head towards the archway to the moors, jerking the bridle from the groom's fingers and galloping away.

"Don't try to jump him, for God's sake!" the groom yelled. Then he dashed into another stable and rode out, bareback, on Andrew's horse, chasing Andrew and Halla as though this was a race with at least a gold cup at stake.

The housekeeper's lips were tight and her face was very white, and Kate asked, because she had to know, "How dangerous is that horse?"

"He's a brute," said the housekeeper shakily, "a devil of a horse."

Kate's blood ran cold. When she had said, "Ride Connor's horse," she hadn't meant Andrew to vault into the saddle and gallop away like the Charge of the Light Brigade. She hadn't meant him to put himself so stupidly at risk.

There were more people in the courtyard now, they looked like staff, and although they all stared at Kate nobody spoke to her. She heard the housekeeper say, "Out of his mind, showing off in front of her," and she ran through the archway to the front of the house to scan the countryside.

She was annoyed with Andrew, this was a childish showoff, but she was also racked with anxiety; and when a horse came galloping over a hill, across the road, down the private track and over the bridge, it was Halla, with no rider on his back, reins and stirrups flapping loose.

The horse came straight for the courtyard, galloping through the archway, hooves clattering on the cobblestones; and then there was a second horse, the groom checking him by dragging on his mane as soon as they were within earshot, yelling, "Get a doctor to Merlin's Cut!" then turning the horse again, and galloping back the way they had come.

Kate knew the Cut. It was a good two miles over rough country, a natural cleft in the turf and a rising of rock like a low wall. Halla could almost certainly have cleared that, but the groom had called, "Don't try to jump him."

Kate began to walk towards the bridge over the stream when she heard her name called, "Kate, Miss Howard!" Mrs. Lammas was standing at the top of the flight of steps to the main door. "What are you doing here? Where's Andrew?"

Kate was alone, and Mrs. Lammas was puzzled. "He went off on Connor's horse," said Kate, and Mrs. Lammas swayed, the colour draining from her face. As Kate ran up the steps Mrs. Shale appeared behind Jennifer Lammas, reaching out to support her, drawing her back into the house.

"It's all right," she was saying as Kate came through the door into the great hall. "You sit down and I'll get your

44

pills. He's all right."

She guided her mistress into the nearest chair and ran into one of the rooms leading off the hall. Jennifer Lammas was fighting for breath, and Kate realised she had a heart condition, and Kate was the one who had broken bad news to her, bluntly and unthinkingly.

Mrs. Shale was back within seconds, and Jennifer Lammas gulped down a couple of pills, then leaned back with closed eyes. When she opened her eyes again her breathing was still fast. "Why did he want to ride Halla?" she gasped.

"Showing off," said Mrs. Shale. "Now, do you feel strong enough to get to a couch?" She put an arm around Jennifer Lammas, and led her into the drawing room, and Kate watched them go with deep concern, wishing she could ask if there was anything she could do, but knowing that if she did Mrs. Shale's reply would be, "You've done enough."

When Mrs. Shale came out of the drawing room she walked across to Kate. "If anything's happened to him," she said, "it'll kill her." She sounded as though Kate was entirely responsible for all this, and Kate couldn't rid herself of the guilty feeling that perhaps she was.

She stayed where she was. The hall was big enough to sit in a chair and pass unnoticed. She wanted to know what had happened to Andrew, but she didn't want to draw attention to herself, she was not among friends.

A man who was obviously a doctor came and Mrs. Lammas went upstairs supported by him and Mrs. Shale. Kate watched them from the shadows, trying to hear what they were saying, they still seemed to be reassuring Mrs. Lammas, when she felt a light touch on her shoulder.

It was Moira, the girl who had brought up Kate's morning tea on Sunday, who said gently, "They've taken him to the General for tests. I'm sure he'll be all right."

She sounded like Mrs. Shale with Mrs. Lammas, and Kate smiled weakly, appreciating Moira's kindness and hoping she was right.

Kate tried to get Susan on the phone, but she had left the hospital and she was on a date. "As soon as she comes in I'll ask her to find out what she can," said Janice, who had taken the call at the flat. "How awful. Poor Andrew!"

"Yes," said Kate. "I'd better hang up. Someone might be trying to get through."

The phone did ring several times, and someone must have answered it promptly because it always stopped after a couple of rings. No one came into the hall to use that extension. Kate sat in the thickening shadows until lights began to be switched on.

When Connor walked through the hall he gave her the briefest of glances and strode upstairs. He didn't say a word to her, but from his expression he knew what had happened, and like the rest of them he blamed her for it. Although if he hadn't kept a horse that was a brute and a devil Andrew couldn't have been thrown today. It was Connor's horse, and it was Andrew's show-off streak, it wasn't all Kate's fault.

She waited, because she couldn't think what else to do. She sometimes asked those who passed through the hall, "Has there been any news?" but they always said there was nothing yet. She didn't see Connor again, but she heard the occasional car coming and going, and stood at the windows, watching the lights. When Mrs. Shale came out on to the gallery, and saw Kate still below, the housekeeper came bustling down the stairs.

"I thought you'd gone hours ago," she said.

"Not yet," said Kate. "Please, do you have any news?"

"Not yet." The housekeeper looked haggard. "But Bert said he couldn't move." She moved away. "I'll get someone to drive you home."

"No," Kate spoke jerkily. "Don't bother. I'll walk."

"Please yourself," said Mrs. Shale.

Kate was deeply shocked and she had to be alone, or with people who wouldn't blame her for the few exasperated words that Andrew had taken so literally. She almost ran from the house; the lights lit her way as far as the stream, but from then on there was only moonlight, and there were clouds hiding the stars and drifting across the moon.

Her thoughts were all of Andrew. She tried to tell herself that it couldn't be as bad as that. He must have been knocked out, so shaken that he was temporarily paralysed. Tomorrow, after a night's rest, he would be on his feet again.

She reached the road without looking back at the house, ahead of her the five-mile walk to Moorton Fells, then another couple of miles to the flat. She shivered as she walked, but less from the night wind than from her thoughts.

She had never walked the moors alone, so late, and if she had not had the ribbon of road to guide her she could have lost her way. The silence—no sound but her own footsteps, her own breathing—the vastness of the dark hills, would have been frightening if she'd let her imagination take over and begun wondering what lurked in the shadows. The lights of the town showed palely on the skyline, but out here she could have been the only human being in the world.

She walked as fast as she dared on the uneven road, and when she saw the car lights coming towards her she got off the road and stood well to the side.

It wasn't too late for cars and anyone walking would probably be offered a lift, but this car was going in the wrong direction, away from town, and anyhow, Kate would have been wary of being picked up in the dark in the middle of the moors.

She recognised the car as it passed her. It was Connor's Mercedes and it was stopping, and she couldn't face Connor Lammas tonight. At that prospect she lost her head completely. The night was a nightmare and she reacted to

47

the dark pursuer of a nightmare. She ran, turning off the road and blundering through the bracken. If she went fast enough he wouldn't follow. She ran as though a killer was at her heels, and when she heard him call "Miss Howard!" she plunged on deeper and ever more wildly.

"Where do you think you're going? Didn't you hear me calling you?" He grabbed at her shoulder and turned her roughly towards him, and she sobbed for breath, straining back from the hands that held her. Her loose dark hair was black in the moonlight and her face was silver pale.

He thought she had panicked because she didn't know who was following her, and she looked up into the hard face and gasped, "I knew it was you." Part of the nightmare, who else would be on the moors tonight?

He was surprised for a moment, then he said grimly, "You'd do well to run from me." He loosed her then, but she still felt his hands on her.

She asked, "How is he?"

"He has a spinal injury."

That could be anything, from a slipped disc to—a broken back. Her lips were dry, although the night air was damp on her skin and her hair. "How bad is it?" she whispered.

"No one knows yet. You got him to ride that horse, didn't you?"

She said dully, "I suppose so, in a way," and flinched at a slight movement from the man.

In his powerful and hooded eyes she could sense a terrifying anger, and an even more terrible danger. He could kill me, she thought. Right here, and no one would know. He could take me away, hide me where no one would find me. Her peril seemed so real to her that she couldn't scream, and for the first time in her life she felt her senses reeling, she was almost fainting from fear.

When he spoke she pulled herself together. He was a civilised cultured man, of course she was in no physical danger. He spoke quietly. "Andrew said, 'I knew I couldn't ride Halla, but Kate thought I could'."

She *was* to blame. Andrew had done it to show her. She almost sobbed, "Oh God!" and Connor said curtly,

"It's a little late for praying." He turned. "I'll have to go home first, then I'll run you back to town."

He meant her to get into the car with him and she couldn't. She was already feeling the flints painfully through the thin soles of her shoes, but she would rather finish up barefoot and bleeding than drive with Connor Lammas. She followed him back to the road, then she said, "I can walk, I don't want—"

"Damn you," he said, "get in. I can't leave even you in the middle of the moors." He held her arm as he opened the door, and he shoved her into the passenger seat, and was round in his seat, and the car was moving before she had her breath back.

There was not one word spoken. Kate sat, with her head down, trying not to see the dark hawklike profile; but she felt every movement of his hands on wheel and gears, the slightest shifting of him beside her, and when the car stopped she fumbled to open her door quickly and get out. She stood in the lights of the courtyard, grateful for the cold wind on her burning face, and Connor Lammas said, "Come on."

She wanted to say, "I'll wait here," but the dampness in the air was turning to rain, so she followed him to the open door where Mrs. Shale met him, giving Kate a sharp look of surprise but with all her attention on Connor and his news from the hospital.

Andrew was comfortable, he told her, and tomorrow all the reports should be in. "How is she?" he asked. He meant his mother.

"She won't go to sleep till she sees you," said Mrs. Shale. "She won't rest until you tell her he's going to be all right."

She smiled faintly. "She thinks you can cure anything."

"Not this time," said Connor.

Mrs. Shale sighed, "No, well, this is a bit beyond all of us." She looked at Kate again and Connor said,

"I'm taking Miss Howard home. Wait here." He meant Kate to wait. Mrs. Shale followed him, and Kate leaned against the wall closing her eyes.

She was feeling the strain in aches and pains by now, and she couldn't even ask them for a headache pill in this house. Everyone here seemed to think she had urged Andrew to ride Halla for kicks, to amuse herself. That was what Connor believed.

He wasn't long, and Kate couldn't ask him how his mother was, but Mrs. Shale had said this could kill her and Kate realised that this might be the worst night of his life. He looked gaunt, the flesh was drawn tight over his face bones, and she said wretchedly, "Oh, I am so sorry."

He looked at her with a contempt that shrivelled, then he said, "Don't apologise to me. I'm walking and my heart's still pumping, but you might have cause to apologise to my family before long. My mother wants to see you."

"Is that—wise?" Surely seeing Kate could only distress Jennifer Lammas, but Connor didn't answer. He turned and she followed him. He never looked back to check she was there, although sometimes she had to hurry to keep up.

The bedroom door was open. Like most of the rooms in this house it was luxurious. In here the lights were shaded and flattering so that a one-time beautiful woman would always be beautiful. The brightest light burned on a table by which a woman sat, doing some sewing.

Jennifer Lammas sat up in bed, pink satin pillows massed behind her, her hair brushed loose. The woman got up when Connor and Kate entered the room, and Mrs. Lammas said, "Thank you, Elsa, I shall be all right now."

She looked very delicate and very sad, and Kate felt that

Andrew's mother might be justified in hating her. His brother did, although heaven knows Kate hadn't meant to hurt anyone. Her voice trembled as she asked, "How are you feeling?" because she could have wept with Mrs. Lammas.

Mrs. Lammas smiled, although her lips were unsteady. "Connor says we can see him tomorrow."

We? She probably meant herself and Connor.

"Andrew is so impulsive," Jennifer Lammas's eyes swam with tears. "It was such a silly thing to do. He could have been—" She touched the lace on the bedjacket at her throat. "Killed," she said in a high scared voice, and although Kate had realised that before it came back to her now and she put a hand before her own eyes. "Come and sit down, my dear," said Mrs. Lammas. "Connor?"

"I think Miss Howard is capable of getting to a chair herself," said Connor. Kate was suddenly aware that her legs were like jelly, but she didn't want Connor Lammas leading her to a chair. She sat down by the little table with the table lamp, and because weakness had hit her suddenly she sat heavily, betraying weariness.

Mrs. Lammas said reproachfully, "At least help her take her coat off," and Kate began to unbutton her coat feverishly fast, but Connor made no move until she was out of it, then he took the few paces between them and held out a hand for her coat, tossing it on to another chair. Mrs. Lammas said, "You're staying the night, of course."

"Me?" stammered Kate. "Mr. Lammas said—he'd take me home."

"I wish you would, dear. I'd like to talk to you."

"But I don't have anything with me," said Kate, hopelessly because that was no excuse, and Connor said shortly,

"Miss Howard will stay."

If Kate could be of any comfort to Mrs. Lammas of course she would stay, but Connor Lammas's calm assumption of

51

command sparked her spirit. She said, "Yes, Mrs. Lammas, I *will* stay," to emphasise that the decision was her own.

"Thank you." Mrs. Lammas settled back again in her pillows. "You're looking very tired."

"I suppose I am." But she was going to find it impossible to stop worrying tonight, and she asked, "Would you have any headache pills? I don't usually get headaches, but I seem to have one now."

"Of course," said Mrs. Lammas with quick sympathy. "Connor, would you look in the top drawer of the bureau?"

Connor opened the top drawer of a French Empire style bureau, looking down, saying, "You don't want a particularly strong drug, I suppose, just a token something?"

Kate gritted her teeth. Was he suggesting she was putting on this show of distress? "An aspirin would be fine," she said coldly, and he brought her a small bottle of aspirins, and poured water into a glass and offered her that too.

She had placed the bottle on the table beside her, but she took the glass awkwardly, trying to avoid touching his hand, so that it tilted as she clutched it and a little water spilt, and she put it down, apologising, "That was clumsy of me."

She brushed the water from her skirt, and Mrs. Lammas smiled at her and said, "Tell me about yourself, Kate."

One pill stuck in Kate's throat and she coughed to get it down. "What—do you want to know?"

Mrs. Lammas had asked her questions on Saturday, but with a polite social smile. She wasn't smiling that way now. Now she said, "Andrew is very fond of you and perhaps I have been old-fashioned. I should like to know you better, Kate."

Kate realised that tonight anything Andrew wanted his mother wished him to have. Kate could be the get-well gift for Mrs. Lammas's son, but this was no time to say, "I don't love Andrew, please leave me alone," and while Kate was wondering what she could say Connor said cynically,

52

"We should all like to know Miss Howard better."

He had taken a chair that was too small for him—all the chairs in this room were. He sat with arms folded and legs stretched in front of him, but he didn't look ridiculous in any way, he still looked dangerous. Kate said bitterly, "You have my dossier. I'm sure that any investigator you employ does a thorough job."

"Oh dear," Mrs. Lammas made a fluttery sigh of that. "Tell me about when you were a little girl," she said. "Did you have a happy childhood?" She wanted to hear Kate's happy memories, but Connor was watching with cold keen eyes. To know her better? To learn her bitter secrets? Kate said tonelessly,

"Childhood is usually happy, isn't it? My parents were killed when I was seventeen."

Mrs. Lammas's face shadowed and she said gently, "That was very sad—and you've been alone ever since? You've had to make your own way?"

It hadn't been hard. It was only Kate's childhood that had been hard. She said, "A lot of girls make their own way these days."

"Oh yes," Mrs. Lammas was quick to agree, "I'm sure they do, these days. You see, I'm old-fashioned, and you're a very modern girl, aren't you, Kate?" She sounded as though Kate was a different species, but if Andrew wanted her Jennifer Lammas was prepared to try to understand her.

Kate said, "I suppose we're all what life makes us." Jennifer Lammas's life had always been gracious, so she was a gracious lady.

"Or what we make of ourselves," said Connor, and his smile was no smile at all. It made even his mother feel a little afraid of him, and he mustn't hurt Kate because Andrew could be in love with her and tonight Andrew could have died.

"Kate," said Jennifer Lammas shakily, "would you like to

see my photographs of Andrew?"

"That would be very nice," said Kate, although her headache was getting worse at a terrifying rate, and Connor got a large velvet-bound album from the bureau. He gave his mother the book and said,

"I'll look in later." He didn't look at Kate until he was at the door and she said,

"Please may I phone my flatmates? They'll be expecting me home." She explained, "I rang through earlier—Susan's a nurse at the General and I thought she might have some news. I tried the hospital first, I thought I might just catch her there, but she'd gone off duty—"

Connor cut in brusquely, "I'll see to it," and she said,

"You'll find the number in the dossier." He couldn't even let her finish her sentence, and she glared at the closed door until Mrs. Lammas said,

"If you'd bring your chair over here, dear."

Kate carried a chair to the bedside table, and, as Mrs. Lammas turned over the first few pages of the album, she found that her headache had miraculously lifted. Either those were the quickest acting aspirins in the world or most of her tension had gone with Connor Lammas.

The first pages must have been before Andrew made his appearance, so they were probably Connor, and Kate asked, "How much older is Connor than Andrew?"

"Seven years," said their mother.

Andrew looked younger than the twenty-eight Kate knew he was, Connor looked older than thirty-five, probably because Connor wielded the power, more on his shoulders, more on his mind. Kate said, "Only seven years?" and Mrs. Lammas agreed,

"It does seem more. It always has. Andrew is young in spirit in a way I don't think Connor ever was. Andrew's like me," she said with satisfaction, "that's why I understand him so well."

54

It was an obvious question. "Don't you understand Connor?"

"Connor doesn't need anyone to understand him," said his mother. "He's always been sufficient unto himself."

There were more pictures of Andrew than Connor. Page after page of Andrew, who really did photograph fantastically well—no wonder he didn't mind getting in front of a camera. The snaps of Connor seemed much more casual, and yet Kate felt that if anyone had come on this record knowing nothing of its background they would have admired Andrew's good looks, but Connor would have made the impact. He looked a man to reckon with, even as a boy.

There was a big handsome jolly-looking man. "My dear husband," sighed Jennifer Lammas. "He died ten years ago." She gave the others who appeared on the photographs names, few of which meant anything to Kate, although she noticed that there were varying girls looking admiringly at Connor.

The girl who figured most often on the pictures with Andrew was Gail Gowerie of Goweries Supermarkets, the girl his mother had wanted him to marry. "They make an attractive pair," said Kate, and Jennifer Lammas sighed, then she closed the book and said,

"Gail is a sweet girl, but Andrew is going to marry for love." She blinked mistily at Kate. "I do believe," she said tremulously, "that what happened today might have been a sign that you and I must get to know each other better." She reached for Kate's hand and now the tears were running down her cheeks. "All I want is Andrew's happiness," she sobbed, "nothing else, and when I think I could have lost him today, really lost him—"

Kate jumped up, taking away the book, begging, "Please don't cry, you mustn't upset yourself; you should be resting."

She wiped away the tears, moistened a handkerchief with

eau de cologne and dabbed Mrs. Lammas's temples, and the sobs ceased and Jennifer Lammas hiccupped, "We'll see him tomorrow, he'll be wanting to see you, Kate—and now if you'll ring the bell for me, dear, we'll both try to get some rest."

Kate's room was exactly the same as last time, the bedside lamp lit, the bed turned down. But it was not Kate's white cotton nightdress on the bed tonight, it was a blue brushed nylon, new and unworn, that must have been loaned by one of the females of the household. Unless, like the toothbrush in the bathroom still in its plastic packaging, they kept these things for overnight guests who arrived with no luggage.

Kate was almost too tired to get ready for bed and she was slumped in a chair when a knock came on the door. She leaped up. "Who is it?"

It was Moira, with a glass of milk and a plate of sandwiches that Kate was sure was her own idea. She said, "Thank you very much."

Moira put them both down on the bedside table, and grinned, "I thought you'd like to know that the hole in the skirting board has been stopped up, so you shouldn't be bothered with mice any more."

"I'd forgotten the mouse." Kate pushed back her heavy hair. "I'd probably have remembered him in the middle of the night and that would have been awful. I'm so glad you told me."

She was glad to see a friendly face too, and she drank the milk, and ate some of the sandwiches although she didn't really feel like food. She was too weary to bath, so she washed her hands and face, and bathed the scratches on her legs and washed out her laddered tights. Then, sitting at the dressing table, she brushed out the tangles from her wind-blown hair. She was back in Connor Lammas's house where everything was his property.

She pulled the nightdress off her shoulder and looked in the mirror. Her skin was white and unmarked. She had wondered if there might be a bruise where he had gripped her and she was relieved there was not. That would have been like carrying a brand.

CHAPTER THREE

KATE slept fitfully and remembered as soon as she woke that this was the day they would learn the extent of Andrew's injuries. She prayed, and she went on praying. She was dressed, looking down into the courtyard and remembering yesterday—Andrew on Halla, calling, "Watch this, Kate"—when Moira came in with her morning tea.

She was glad it was Moira, who said, "I'd have brought your tea up earlier, miss, but I didn't think you'd be awake yet," and then asked, "Didn't you sleep so good?"

"On and off," said Kate.

"Mr. Lammas is up, he's always an early riser." Moira put down the tray and poured the tea. "Mrs. Lammas is having breakfast in her room this morning, and she said would you join her there?" She offered Kate her cup of tea and asked, "Did you know you've got a hole in your tights, miss?"

It was a broad ladder and a large hole, and Kate said ruefully, "I started to walk to town last night and I snagged them." She could hardly admit that she'd done it running from Connor Lammas, and she finished, "Then Mr. Lammas passed me in the car and brought me back here."

"I could let you have a pair," Moira offered.

"I'd be very grateful if you would." The only make-up Kate had with her was a lipstick. Nothing to disguise her pallor or the blue shadows round her eyes. She looked waif-like enough without a great hole in her tights, and when Moira returned with a new pair she said, "Bless you, I'll replace these as soon as I get back to civilisation. By the way, where did the nightdress come from?"

"From Mrs. Shale," said Moira. "She'd bought it for her sister's birthday next week."

Kate allowed herself a faint grin. "If I'd known I'd never have dared to wear it. I do hope somebody replaces it, I daren't offer," and Moira smiled too.

Mrs. Lammas was still in bed, when Kate tapped on her door and was told to come in. Her hair was smoothly brushed and she looked more rested than Kate felt, but she had probably been given sleeping pills. She had a little bed-table across her knees, with fruit juice and a boiled egg. She was sipping the fruit juice and she smiled at Kate and told her, "Andrew had a very good night."

"I'm so glad," said Kate.

"Sit down, dear, they'll bring your breakfast up. We have to wait until this afternoon before we can see him, but perhaps we'll be bringing him home with us then."

This was very different from the last breakfast Kate had taken with Jennifer Lammas. A tray was brought in for Kate and she sat at a little table, eating her egg and toast fingers, with Andrew's mother looking at her approvingly. Jennifer Lammas was deciding that something might be made of Kate Howard, if Andrew really was serious and Connor would show a little tolerance. The girl had quite an air of distinction, she was not in the least like the last one, thank goodness.

Jennifer Lammas talked of Andrew all through breakfast: boyhood escapades, what he liked and what he disliked, every illness he had had from mumps on Christmas Day at the age of seven to a leg broken on the St. Moritz slopes the year before last. If Kate had been in love with Andrew she would have found it enthralling. As it was she found it touching. He was the light of his mother's life, and the bulletin from the hospital this morning had been good and Kate was so thankful about that that she listened willingly and happily.

After they had both eaten breakfast Kate went down into the breakfast room. It wasn't nine o'clock yet, but she should phone Angus and explain where she was. The news of Andrew's accident would have been relayed to the store, and Kate would have liked to go in to work this morning and go round to the hospital during visiting hours this afternoon. If someone would run her back to Moorton Fells.

But Mrs. Lammas had gone on talking about Andrew until Kate finished her last piece of toast, then she had said, "I'll see you downstairs in the breakfast room in about half an hour, my dear," and so Kate had gone downstairs.

She found the breakfast room, and it was empty, and she sat there hoping that Mrs. Lammas would come in before Connor. If Connor was still in the house. If he made a habit of early rising he probably started work early, and after he had checked Andrew's progress he might have left for an office somewhere.

She waited until she heard a phone ring, and shortly afterwards Mrs. Shale came in to say, "A call for you, miss."

"Thank you." That would very likely be Janice or Susan, and Kate hurried after Mrs. Shale to the nearest phone extension, in a room that looked like a study. A connecting door was open into a much bigger room with book-lined walls. The phone was on a green-leather-topped desk, and the voice was Susan's.

"Kate? You wanted me to ring you, didn't you?"

"Oh yes," said Kate. "Do you have any news?"

"Only what Mr. Lammas knows already—Connor Lammas. The X-rays don't show much, but the nervous system could be damaged and it could be a long job. He doesn't seem to have any feeling at all in his legs."

Shock took Kate's breath and she stammered, "But—he had a good night."

"Yes, he did," said Susan. "But he was sedated."

"But his mother thinks he's doing fine. She thinks he'll be leaving hospital this afternoon."

Susan sounded dubious. "He might be leaving quite soon,

I'm sure he could be nursed at Lammas Knowle, but he's very far from fine." She sighed for him. "Poor Andrew doesn't have much luck, does he?"

"It's terrible," Kate whispered.

"It is," Susan agreed. "Has this—well, has it changed how you feel about him?"

"I feel as though I'm to blame," Kate said raggedly. "He'd never ridden that horse before. I gave him the idea of riding it, I made it a sort of challenge," and she heard Susan's soft comforting voice,

"Oh, Kate, how awful for you, but you couldn't have known—"

"But I did know the horse was dangerous, I did know that, but I didn't think this would happen." She wanted to talk to Susan as she had wanted to get to Susan and Janice last night, because they would have understood, but there was a movement in the doorway that led from the library and she looked round to see Connor Lammas. "I'll have to go now, Sue," she said. "I'll see you later."

"You are all right?" Susan was anxious.

"Yes," said Kate, "I'm all right." She put down the phone and asked indignantly, "Do you often listen in to other people's phone calls?"

Connor Lammas came into the room, elegant, immaculate, cold as charity. "Your friend the nurse at the General?" he said.

"Yes." He must have realised what Sue had been telling her. "But Mrs. Lammas thinks—" Kate began, and he cut her short, speaking quickly and concisely.

"I know what Mrs. Lammas thinks, but this has to be broken to her gently. All she needs to know at the moment is that Andrew had a restful night, and we can bring him home as soon as arrangements have been made."

"I see."

"I hope you do." That was said grimly, almost like a

threat, and she asked,

"May I go to work now?"

"They know where you are. As my mother seems to be finding some comfort in your company I'd prefer you to stay here until this afternoon."

They stood, facing each other. Kate was tallish for a girl, but Connor was well above average height for a man, and she found herself stretching her spine and neck as though being looked down on put her at a disadvantage. "Very well," she said, and turned on her heel and went back to the breakfast room.

Mrs. Lammas was there now and Kate explained, "One of the girls I live with just phoned me."

"Ah, the nurse?" Jennifer Lammas's face brightened with interest. "What did she have to tell you?"

"That Andrew had had a good night." That was true, and when Jennifer Lammas looked disappointed, asking,

"Nothing else?" Kate said,

"I don't think he's on her ward. Oh, and I spoke to Connor and he suggested I stay here until this afternoon."

"But of course you must," Jennifer Lammas said firmly. "Then we can all go and see Andrew together."

Kate spent the morning with Andrew's mother, quietly, although the phone rang often, and they ate lunch together in a dining room that was small by Lammas Knowle standards, while Jennifer Lammas did the talking. She was buoyed up by the thought of seeing Andrew this afternoon, but Kate was dreading it.

Connor drove them, and Kate sat huddled in the back of the car. She had been taken to the General Hospital after the car crash in which her parents died. She remembered the layout of the building, the all-pervading antiseptic smell, and she felt very much now as she had felt then, alone and sick and frightened.

Connor Lammas opened the car door for her in the car

park, but after that he took no notice of her at all. Neither did Mrs. Lammas; she was only intent on getting to Andrew. Kate could have slipped away and done her visiting later, but now she was here that would have been cowardly. So she followed some way behind, wondering if she might get a glimpse of Susan or anyone else she knew.

Through Susan she did know several of the staff, but today she saw no friends, and when they reached Andrew's room Mrs. Lammas hurried in, Connor just behind her, and Kate so far behind that the door swung to after them, and she had to open it again.

It was a small room and Andrew's was the only bed, and when Kate stepped in Mrs. Lammas was blinking away tears and telling Andrew what a silly thing that was to do, and did he have any idea how much worry he had caused? She leaned over to touch his hair and his face with little patting petting caresses, as though he was still the small boy or the beautiful baby.

Andrew didn't look too bad, he looked tired, but he moved his head and shoulders, and when he saw Kate coming into the room he said, "You brought Kate," sounding pleased.

"Kate and I have been making friends." Mrs. Lammas held out her hand for Kate, and drew the girl forward to stand beside her so that Kate really did feel like an offering, a get-well gift. She said,

"Hello," at a loss for words. It was hard to say how grieved she was to see him here while Connor watched impassively. She couldn't ask him how he was because she knew how he was and it was a forbidden subject.

Andrew spoke first. "I couldn't ride him after all, could I, Kate? but I'll soon be on my feet again. You don't have to jilt me because of this."

His mother said sharply, "Stop teasing. Of course Kate isn't going to leave you."

"Are you, Kate?" It wasn't fair of Andrew to blackmail her like this, but he was waiting for her answer, and it seemed that Connor was too. Connor hadn't spoken, but she could feel his eyes on her. She tried to smile and said,

"You hurry up and get well."

"I'll do that," said Andrew, as though she had made a condition and he was accepting it.

It was a short visit. Connor talked briefly about Andrew coming home soon, and after that Mrs. Lammas chattered brightly about plans that showed she expected him to be back to normal in next to no time. Kate said nothing. She just sat there, until Connor said they had better be going.

"Not already, surely?" his mother protested, but her cheeks were flushed and Connor said,

"I think so." Andrew looked at him with a sudden flash of desperate appeal and Connor said quietly, "Don't worry, old lad, it'll be all right."

"Goodbye," murmured Kate. She felt that she had no right to be watching Connor's reassurances for Andrew, or his mother's goodbyes, and she slipped out of the room while Mrs. Lammas was kissing Andrew and promising that she would be back tomorrow.

Kate had hardly moved from the door before Connor came out. "Miss Howard," he said.

She backed another couple of steps. "I'm going in to work now."

"You've got leave of absence."

"Why?"

"I'll see you in your flat in about an hour."

"*Why?*"

"Just be there." He opened the door of Andrew's room again, waiting for Mrs. Lammas, and Kate began to hurry down the corridor, almost running, as she had done on the moors trying to escape, but taking with her a shuddering premonition of darkness.

It was a fine day, but a black depression was on her, and Kate was not easily depressed. She had a resilient spirit, but going inside that hospital again had brought back memories; and seeing Andrew like that had been distressing; and the thought of going home and waiting for Connor Lammas chilled her blood.

What could he have to say to her that he couldn't have said at Lammas Knowle? One thing was sure, Mrs. Lammas might have softened towards Kate since Andrew's accident, but Connor Lammas had not. And he had heard her on the phone this morning, admitting to Susan that she had challenged Andrew to ride Halla, although she knew the horse was dangerous.

She walked back home, instead of catching a bus. The exercise didn't lift her depression, but it warmed her blood and cut down the waiting time for Connor Lammas.

She let herself into the flat, lit the oil radiator, turned on a bar of the electric fire, and made herself a strong coffee. She didn't want to start shivering no matter what he said to her, and she was in two minds whether to take a glass of cheap red plonk. But she decided against that. She wasn't so much in awe of Connor Lammas that she needed Dutch courage to face him. She wasn't in awe of him at all, she simply disliked him intensely. So much so that when the front door bell rang, at about the time she was expecting him, she clapped her hands over her ears to shut out the sound, screwed her eyes tight and stood quite still, like a small child hoping something horrid will go away.

Instead of which there was a knock on the door at the top of the steps, which meant that someone else had answered the bell and the caller was for Kate. It was Connor. She opened the door and said, "Come in," then walked down again into the living room with its bright cheap junk furnishings, and the emulsion paint mural on the wall.

Kate liked this room. They had had fun getting the bits

and pieces together, and they had fun living here. She was in no way ashamed of it, and Connor Lammas gave nothing a second glance. He followed Kate down and stood looking at her, but somehow her pride was stung as though he had summed up every item, and she had to bite her lip to stop herself from saying, "Yes, it is trash, you'd chop it up and use it for firewood in Lammas Knowle. But we painted it and we like it, and maybe trash is in the eye of the beholder because that's how you look at me and you don't know the first thing about me." What she did say was, "Won't you sit down?"

"No, thank you," he said. They were standing facing each other again, and she said challengingly,

"All right, what do we have to discuss this time?"

"You seem to be having second thoughts about taking on a cripple." He said that so calmly that she could hardly believe her ears, then she croaked,

"What an unspeakably foul thing to say!"

"Am I wrong?" he said curtly.

"Are you wrong?" She was blazing now. "This will come as the surprise of your life, you never think you could be wrong, do you? but you've been wrong about this from the beginning. I never wanted to marry Andrew."

He smiled slowly, cynically. "Which is an emphatic way of saying that you don't now, and I'm not in the least surprised. A girl like you could always get a better offer than a man who might be helpless, even if he is comparatively wealthy."

Anger so scorching that she lost control had never happened to her before. She had longed more than once to hit out at him, but those had been impulses she could resist and this was a reflex action. It just happened. She would have struck him full in the face, if his reactions had been slower, but he caught her wrist and held it upraised in a grip of steel.

She didn't struggle. She was appalled at the advantage she had given him. She had just acted idiotically and they both knew it. The fire and fury went out of her and her voice was flat and bitter.

"I'm sorry for Andrew, I always was sorry for him—he can't call his soul his own, can he? You were a giant, he said, towering over him in everything. That was why he tried to ride your horse, to prove he was as good a rider as you."

He loosed her wrist. It ached and she wanted to rub it, but she let her hand fall to her side, as though there had been no violence between them. "To prove to you that he was as good a rider," said Connor.

"Well—yes."

"There's a good chance he'll recover."

She was so thankful to hear thath. Her "Thank heaven!" came in a deep sigh of relief. Then she realised there was more, he hadn't finished, and her lips stiffened and she raised wary eyes to him. He said,

"But a great deal depends on his own efforts. If you walk out on him now he could take it as proof that he's permanently crippled."

She couldn't understand what this was leading to. "You're not suggesting I marry him?"

"Not so long as I can stand in your way," said Connor.

"That's what I thought. What then?"

"If you go now it's possible he never will walk again. Andrew's no fighter, he could give up very easily. As you're responsible for what happened to him yesterday I think the least you can do is stay until some of the damage is repaired."

"Stay?" She latched on to the word. "What do you mean by stay?"

"In Lammas Knowle. If you're near him, encouraging him to walk, it could give him the incentive."

67

"Live in your house?" She sounded as though she was being strangled. "With you?"

"In my house," he said impatiently, "but hardly with me," and she turned away to hide her face that had flushed hot. She wanted to say no, and go on saying no, but Connor Lammas wouldn't be harbouring her under his roof unless it could mean all the difference to Andrew's chances of walking again. And much of the blame was hers, and she couldn't refuse anything that might help.

She said quietly, "I've no choice. I'll come."

"Thank you. We shall be taking Andrew home on Sunday. Until then you can either come back to Lammas Knowle or stay here, but I suggest that you go and see him tomorrow."

"I'll stay here, and of course I'll visit him."

"I'll call for you on Sunday."

She said quickly, "Don't bother, I'd rather make my own way."

"As you always do." But now she was going his way, she was a prisoner again. And so was Andrew until he could walk, and it was Andrew she should feel sorry for, not herself. Although she would almost rather have been going to prison than going to live in Connor Lammas's home.

"Good afternoon," he said.

As soon as his back was turned she instinctively rubbed her wrist, watching the tall broad-shouldered figure walking up the steps to the door. If she had actually hit him would that have shattered his calm? He had held off the blow and dropped her hand as though he was brushing a leaf from his jacket. It hadn't even interrupted the conversation.

She thought, a little hysterically, another time I must move faster, and Connor turned at the top of the steps. "There had better not be another time," he said. The coincidence silenced her. It was as though he had read her thoughts. She gasped, and he went.

Then she looked around the bright room and missed it

68

even before she had left it. She had shared other rooms with other girls, but this was the first unfurnished flat where they had really imprinted their personalities. The other girls had been friends, most of them were friends still, but with Susan and Janice the relationship had grown into something almost sisterly.

Why couldn't she go on living here, and stay on at work, and spend her evenings and weekends with Andrew? Why hadn't she suggested that to Connor? Because if she had he would have said it wasn't enough. It was the day-to-day, hour-by-hour companionship that Andrew needed, with Kate beside him, to encourage him to make the effort to walk again. Once Andrew had recovered she would be free, but until then she must stay at Lammas Knowle or her conscience would give her no peace for the rest of her life.

Janice was the first home and she listened, looking grave. "How do you really feel about it?" she asked, when Kate finished by explaining what she had agreed to do.

"What choice do I have?" Kate asked, and when Susan arrived from work at the hospital she backed up what Connor Lammas had said. They were still doing tests on Andrew Lammas, but his own strength of spirit could be the vital factor in how soon he walked again. Or even if he walked again.

"He's got to walk again." Janice was dealing with fish fingers and frozen chips in the kitchenette, and Kate had been laying the table when Susan arrived. Kate gave up her task and moved restlessly around the room. "He's *got* to," she repeated, because anything else was too terrible to think about.

"Then, when he's better, you'll leave him?" Susan inquired.

"And come back here if you'll have me," said Kate. "Connor said I was on leave of absence, so I must be getting some of my salary, so I can go on paying my share of the rent. I'll come back and then I'll get myself another job locally."

"You might not want to leave Lammas Knowle," said Susan in her soft sweet voice. "You might even fall in love with Andrew."

Kate had her back to them, facing the wall on which she had painted her mural, 'Space'. Maybe she could paint a wall in her bedroom at Lammas Knowle and fool herself she wasn't closed in. "I won't fall in love with Andrew," she said emphatically, "but I could very easily end up murdering Connor."

She turned and pulled a face, and they grinned faintly with her. "It's a big house," said Janice, tipping in the second batch of frozen chips with an immense splutter. "You should be able to keep out of his way."

"I should," Kate agreed. But she remembered that Connor Lammas had found her in the picture gallery, and on the moors walking home, and she had a crazy frightening feeling that perhaps he could find her anywhere.

When Kate called at the hospital to see Andrew next day Mrs. Lammas was there, with a woman who had worn a blue velvet dress at the dinner party. Now Mrs. Fanshawe wore a beautiully cut suit, and when Mrs. Lammas said, "You've met Kate haven't you? Kate's coming to stay with us for a while," Mrs. Fanshawe smiled knowingly.

Andrew was delighted about the arrangement, and today there was colour in his face so that he looked almost himself again, and Kate felt sure it wouldn't be long before he was walking. Then there would be the problem of telling him that she had stayed from friendship, not from love, and that she still had no intention of marrying him. But first things first, and all that mattered right now was getting him back on his feet.

She left before his mother and Mrs. Fanshawe did, and

Andrew held her hand tight and said, "I'll see you at home tomorrow."

"At Lammas Knowle." It wasn't her home, it was just the place she had to be. "About tea time," she said.

"A charming girl," said Eleanor Fanshawe when Kate had left. She knew how worried Jennifer had been about Andrew and the girl from the store, but the accident had changed everything. Now Andrew couldn't be crossed, and the girl was striking to look at. Quiet, but undoubtedly attractive.

One of the first things I shall do, Jennifer Lammas was musing, is get her some new clothes. She would look quite elegant in some really good clothes. And perhaps her hair could be styled. It would be enjoyable moulding Kate into Andrew's life-style, decided his mother, and helping them both to a fairy tale ending of happy-ever-after.

A boy-friend of Janice's gave Kate a lift to Lammas Knowle. Janice came too and when they reached the turning off the main track Kate said, "Put me down here, please, I'll walk the rest. If I'm delivered to the door I might panic and ask you to drive off with me fast."

The great house, in its setting of rocks and water, looked magnificent, and the young man grinned, "I wouldn't say no to a holiday there."

"It's a big house," said Janice, as she had said on Friday night, and Kate gave a rueful smile while she tried to sound flippant.

"I've got this thing about castles. I'm sure they've all got dungeons." She climbed out with her case. "Thanks, John," she said to the boy-friend, and to Janice, " 'Bye. I'll phone you both and I'll be back as soon as I can. I'll miss you and our flat."

She began to walk down the drive, towards the bridge over the stream, and John asked Janice, "Does she mean that, she'll be back as soon as she can?"

"She means it," said Janice.

71

Kate needed to be alone for a few minutes before she knocked on the door of Lammas Knowle. It was a fine afternoon. Early rain had left the ground soggy, but everything seemed fresh and clean, and she walked slowly. The main door was closed, there was no sign of life at the front of the house, but through that archway, in the courtyard, there would be activity.

As a picture it was serene and strong and she thought—maybe I'll have some time for painting while I'm here. I could paint the house, the moors. She stood for a few moments on the bridge looking at the house; and at the lake with the tiny island, and the round summerhouse with a dome for a roof, standing among the trees. She had wanted to cross to the summerhouse last time she was here, just a week ago. Well, she would get her chance in the days to come. Maybe, she thought crazily, they'd let me move in there. I'd rather live on the island than in the house. Then she picked up her case and walked on.

There were people in the courtyard. The top of Halla's stable door was open and the groom came out of an adjacent stable, noting Kate and raising a hand. She half waved back, and wondered if Halla was still here. After Andrew's accident Mrs. Lammas would probably be fiercely prejudiced against the horse. She wondered if Connor had sent it away.

She knocked on the door that led into the corridor past the kitchens and Elsa, the woman who had been sewing in Mrs. Lammas's room answered. She was stoutly built and florid of face and middle-aged, and she said, "Come in, miss, they are expecting you," quite amiably. Then she looked beyond Kate, and seeing no transport asked, "How did you come?"

"Friends brought me," Kate explained. "I walked from the road."

"Ah yes—well, Mr. Lammas wanted to see you as soon as you got here."

"Which Mr. Lammas?" Kate asked.

"The master." That could only be Connor. "So if you'll leave your case we'll take it up to your room, and I'll take you along."

"Thank you," said Kate.

Connor Lammas was in the study, sitting at the green-topped desk, with a pen in his hand, an open file in front of him, and Kate swallowed the jeer, "Investigated anyone interesting lately?" because she wouldn't make her stay here any more tolerable by provoking Connor Lammas. He said, "I won't keep you long, Andrew's anxious to see you. He wasn't sure you'd come."

"But you were?"

"Yes."

"And this time you were right." The pen was dull gold. He laid it down and she asked, "And what are my conditions of employment?"

"That was what I wanted to see you about." He obviously agreed that her position here was employee, not guest. "The same salary you were getting in Publicity?"

"And free board and lodging?"

"Of course."

"You're too kind." He didn't have to answer that, his expression was as sardonic as her voice. "So what are my duties?" she asked. "Am I a nurse?"

"Are you?"

She shrugged. "I've nursed things like 'flu and sprained ankles. Nothing spectacular."

"There's a full-time nurse in attendance," he said. "And a physiotherapist coming in daily. You're here to keep telling Andrew he's going to walk again, and sound as though it matters to you."

Of course it mattered to her. Did he think she was totally unfeeling?

"It matters," she said, adding cuttingly, "And then I can

73

get out of here and away from you. Is that all?"

"That's all." He stood up and went towards the door with long strides and she turned too, reaching for the doorknob as he did, so that their hands brushed and she snatched hers away as though she had been scalded, and he said curtly,

"Don't worry. When I said you were a girl who'd always get a better offer I didn't mean from me."

"When I said you couldn't meet my price I meant that," she drawled. She got out of the room, closing the door behind her, and steadied herself, then swallowed to get rid of the constriction in her throat. She must stop panicking like this, flinching at a casual touch, or the man might begin to believe she was afraid of him.

Andrew's bed had been moved into a downstairs room that overlooked the front of the house. It didn't look like a sickroom, it looked like a sitting room except for the bed, and Mrs. Lammas was in a chair by the window, reading out extracts from a newspaper.

When Elsa opened the door to admit Kate Kate heard Andrew grumbling, "For God's sake, Mother, there's nothing wrong with my eyes," and Mrs. Lammas was saying,

"You don't want to tire yourself, dear. You only came out of hospital today, remember." Then she saw Kate and cried, "Ah, Kate, how lovely!" and came to greet Kate with open arms, enfolding her in a scented embrace, while Andrew said,

"I've been waiting for you, Kate. Do tell my mother that if I want to know the news I can still read a newspaper."

"Oh, we're going to have our hands full with him!" Mrs. Lammas smiled at Kate as though they were united for Andrew's recovery, as indeed they were. "He's always been a handful when he wasn't well." She went on archly, "Now I'm sure I've got something to discuss with Nurse," and she went smiling out of the room.

"That," said Andrew, "is so that you can kiss me." Kate thought so too. She kissed him briefly on the cheek and he

74

caught her arm.

"It isn't contagious," he said. "You won't catch anything." He pulled her back, and kissed her lips, and after a moment she raised her head.

"I don't kiss well to order," she said.

Andrew went on smiling. "They won't be back for a while."

He thought that was what was inhibiting her, and she couldn't say that her kiss was no more than a gesture of affection and sympathy. She asked, "How are you feeling today? You're looking better."

"I made a mess of it, didn't I?" He tapped his leg with a clenched fist, his expression showing there was no feeling there, and Kate said quickly,

"Perhaps it wasn't a good idea, but you're going to be all right. Most of it is up to you, but this is something I know you can do."

He looked thoughtful, then he brightened. "My mother likes you. I told you she would."

"If she does," said Kate gaily, "I hope she'll find me something to do while I'm here. I can't just sit around."

"You can talk to me."

There was a touch of petulance in his voice, and she went to the window, looking out across the moors. You couldn't see the lake, that was at the side of the house, but you could see the bridge that Kate had crossed less than half an hour ago, and the road. A car was turning now from the road.

"I can't talk to you all the time," said Kate, "you'd get sick of the sound of my voice."

"I would not."

"Well, I would, so somebody will have to find me something to do." She watched the car and decided it was a Rolls-Royce, and Andrew said,

"You could try to win Connor over."

"That's beyond me. I know when I'm beaten, and your

brother is never going to like me." She laughed, but Andrew wasn't treating it as a joke. He said very seriously,

"Of course he will, Kate, when he gets to know you like I do."

"You think so?" she murmured, watching the car slow down to cross the bridge. But Andrew only knew the way she looked and talked and moved, he knew nothing of the real Kate. Less even than Connor who had seen her self-control snap, something she would not let happen again.

"What are you watching?" Andrew asked sharply, almost suspiciously.

"Someone's coming. Who do you know with a Rolls-Royce?"

"Oh, several folk," he said moodily, and Kate laughed again.

"Ask a silly question," she said.

The visitors were Gail Gowerie and her mother. When Mrs. Lammas introduced Kate to Mrs. Gowerie Kate got a frosty look, but Gail didn't seem to be bearing any malice. "We've met, haven't we, Kate?" she said, and to Andrew, "Welcome home, this is better than the grisly old hospital." She pulled up a chair for herself beside his bed and began to give him messages from friends.

Kate said softly, "I'll go and do my unpacking," and Mrs. Lammas nodded and smiled at her.

She had the same room, and she went up to it through the picture gallery. She would have time now to look at the pictures, and she rushed her unpacking and went back into the gallery, where she wandered up and down, as enraptured as Aladdin in the cave of treasures.

When Mrs. Shale came searching for her, to tell her the visitors had left and Andrew was asking for her, Kate confessed, "I didn't realise how time was going," and hurried downstairs to find Andrew alone with Mrs. Lammas. A tea tray on a table looked as though the callers had had tea before they went.

"Where have you been, Kate?" he demanded fretfully. "You can't have been unpacking all this while."

"I was in the picture gallery."

"Well, don't run away like that again." If he had not been lying there helpless she would have resented that, because it was said as though she was guilty of a misdemeanour, but in the circumstances she apologised, and Mrs. Lammas announced soothingly,

"Nurse thinks we should have an early night."

"Nurse thinks *I* should have an early night," said Andrew.

"That's what I said, dear," said his mother. "And I have some letters to write and perhaps Kate would like to watch television, so we'll both say goodnight."

She kissed her son tenderly, and Kate kissed him lightly, and as they went out the nurse bustled in. "Poor boy," sighed Jennifer Lammas. "It's very hard on him."

Kate realised that. It was understandable that Andrew should be irritable, and she was sorry she hadn't come straight downstairs from her unpacking. But she wasn't sorry he was having an early night. "Is there anything I can do?" she asked Mrs. Lammas, who blinked and said,

"For me? No, thank you, dear. You go and watch television and I'll have some tea sent in to you, although we shall be having dinner at seven."

It was almost six now and Kate said, "I'll wait until dinner, thank you. Would you mind if I went for a walk in the garden?"

"Of course not. This is your home, you can go where you like." She patted Kate's arm, and went off across the great hall while Kate ran to fetch a coat. She could find her way to her room now, the size of Lammas Knowle still seemed weird, but she was learning her way around. She came down again into the great hall and let herself out through the main door.

77

It was quite light still, a pleasant evening, and she wanted to see inside the little summerhouse on the little island. No one seemed to be around out here, and she walked round the edge of the lake, which the waterfall fed, feeling the spray on her face. The lawns led to the water's edge and the bridge was very narrow, with only room for one to cross at a time. It was made of wrought iron, and beneath it the water seemed quite deep and fairly fast moving. The turf on the island was cropped short, and the summerhouse stood in a copse of about a dozen trees.

Kate half expected the door to be locked, but it wasn't, and she pushed it open with a thrill of anticipation. Inside was cool; not 'damp as a ditch' as Andrew had said, just cool and very peaceful and quiet. There were four narrow windows in the circular wall, glass-covered and clean enough to see through. A stone seat ran around the wall, there was no furniture, and when Kate knelt on the seat and looked out of a window, across the lake towards the river and the hills, she had the most wonderful sensation of security and isolation, as though no one could hurt her here. She could almost believe there was no bridge, that she was safe and alone on an island that no one else could reach.

It wasn't going to be easy living at Lammas Knowle. Connor would be a watchful jailer and Andrew a demanding invalid. Just now when Andrew had wailed, "Where have you been, Kate? Don't run away like that again," she had heard echoes of her childhood and her mother's complaining whine if Kate, even as a girl of seventeen, was out of her sight without every minute being accounted for.

In that unhappy home Kate would read voraciously, moving into the story. Or draw pictures, and imagine herself part of the picture, shutting her ears and eyes and senses to the sound of raised voices and banging doors. She had invented her islands of escape as a child, but this island was real, she could escape here any time and draw strength from its timeless peace. It was a secret place. Andrew didn't care for it, and she couldn't imagine Connor wasting time listening to lapping water or looking at the view. She was safe here, and after a while she felt calm enough to face the meal ahead at Connor Lammas's table.

Moira served dinner and Kate was glad to see her. She had Moira's pair of replacement tights in her room, but this didn't seem the time to mention that, so she just smiled and said, "Hello," and Moira smiled demurely back.

For most of the meal Kate was smiling demurely too, as Mrs. Lammas did the talking. Connor spoke when spoken to, obviously considering himself superior to female prattle. As Kate didn't speak to him he didn't speak to her, but Mrs. Lammas talked all the time. About Andrew, about their friends, about plans for the days ahead. "Will you come shopping with me one day, Kate?" she asked, and Kate said,

"I'd like to," eating her sweet, a delicious but rather sickly concoction with a lot of cream. Connor had had cheese, which hadn't surprised Kate.

"I need some new clothes," said Mrs. Lammas, exquisitely dressed as always, "and I'm sure you could find a use for some pretty dresses."

Kate liked clothes. She was always ready to buy something new if the funds stretched to it, but Mrs. Lammas sounded as though she was considering a spending spree and Kate said, "I wouldn't mind buying a new dress, but nothing too expensive."

Mrs. Lammas laughed merrily. "Oh, you mustn't let that bother you, my dear. I know just the place, I've an account there, and I should love to help you choose lots of pretty things."

Put them on her account, she meant, and it could well be Connor who settled when the bills came in. "I think I'd better stick to the shops I know," said Kate. "It's very kind

79

of you, but I'll just buy one dress. I don't need any more."

"We'll see." Jennifer Lammas was sure that Kate could be persuaded into accepting the clothes she would need if she was going to do Andrew credit, and Kate let it go at that. She couldn't argue in front of Connor, but she was adamant that no one was giving her gifts under the delusion that she was a future Mrs. Lammas. So far as she could she was staying her own woman, and taking advantage of Jennifer Lammas would have been dishonest.

That evening they sat together in the drawing room. Connor had vanished after dinner, and Jennifer Lammas looked at Kate with shining eyes and said, "I always wanted a daughter. Andrew is the dearest boy, and Connor has always been a tower of strength, but I always longed for a daughter."

"With two sons," said Kate, "you stand a good chance of getting two daughters."

"One at any rate." Jennifer Lammas looked as though she was content with Kate as a candidate and Kate felt Connor should have explained that there was no chance of that. She was here under false pretences but surely the only one who had to be deceived for a while, for his own good, was Andrew. "I'm beginning to realise that Connor is a born bachelor," sighed Jennifer Lammas.

Kate asked, "You mean a woman-hater?" and his mother laughed,

"Goodness, no, he's had some very nice girl-friends. Beautiful girls."

She viewed their passing with regret. "Several times I've thought it was serious, but he doesn't seem to want to get married."

Kate was thinking she wouldn't wish Connor Lammas on any woman, but she supposed he was a man who did appeal to women. There were few very rich men who didn't, and at face value he was physically attractive. Well, she supposed he was, to most women.

"He'll be in Zürich all next week," said Jennifer Lammas, and Kate's smile broadened. With Connor out of the way she could walk around the house without the fear of meeting him round the next corner, she could go into the library and browse through the books without being scared that the study door might open. She could even eat her meals without risk of choking.

"By next weekend," said Mrs. Lammas, "Andrew should be much better."

But Andrew was not, except that he was out of bed and into a wheelchair for most of the day. The muscles in his legs had so far failed to respond, although these were early days, said the nurse, and they would, with patience and perseverance.

Visitors came. Gail came daily, but Andrew insisted on Kate staying in close attendance, enjoying having her at his beck and call, although there was always that reserve in Kate that he couldn't reach, something held back. She hurried to answer his every whim, she helped the nurse, and his mother had started to use her as companion-cum-secretary. Kate was becoming a boon to the household staff, but Andrew still wasn't sure he really had her, and she wouldn't walk out on him.

Her only escape was for an hour or two in the afternoons, during massage and exercise time, which she usually passed in the summerhouse. If she could have taken a long walk across the moors that would have been marvellous, but she knew there would have been a fuss if she had left the grounds, where there was nowhere like the little island for refreshing her spirit. After she had been alone in the summerhouse for a while she could go back to Andrew, to try to cheer him up and promise him he would soon be walking again.

"I will," he'd say, "for you."

"For yourself," she'd say. But the first week passed with

no progress, and she was going home for the weekend, to the flat she shared with Sue and Janice, and Andrew was none too pleased about that. He did his best to make her feel guilty for deserting him, and she was nearly pressured into staying.

"What are you going to do?" he cross-questioned her. "Who will you be seeing?"

"I want to see Sue and Janice," she explained as patiently as she could. "I'll be back on Sunday evening." And because she really needed that break she stayed firm. She was being driven into Moorton Fells on Friday afternoon in the Range Rover, but Connor's car drew up in the courtyard while she was at the window of her bedroom just after lunch.

She watched him get out, open a garage door and drive in. Then she saw him crossing the courtyard towards the house, talking to the groom and another man. Suddenly he looked up and she stepped back quickly from the window; she would have hated him to catch her watching him.

She had hoped to be gone before he returned, but now he was here she supposed she should go and ask him to tell his mother that she was not a prospective daughter-in-law. If that could be settled while Kate was out of Lammas Knowle the fuss should be over by Sunday night, and as Jennifer Lammas was set on matchmaking she could return to Gail. Gail's constant visits showed that she was still very fond of Andrew.

The physiotherapist was with Andrew now, Mrs. Lammas was resting in her room, and Kate waited for about half an hour before trying to speak to Connor in private. She didn't want a tête-à-tête, she wanted to keep right away from him, but she went into the kitchen and asked Mrs. Shale where she could find him.

Mrs. Shale was nicer to Kate these days, and she told her that Connor was in the study, so Kate tapped on the study door.

"Come in," he called. "Oh," he said, sitting behind the desk when she walked in, "it's you."

"Sorry about that," she said crisply, "but your mother is brainwashing herself that I'm her future daughter-in-law, and I wish you'd explain the set-up."

"Sorry, I can't do that." He stroked his chin. "I couldn't rely on her not bursting into tears and telling Andrew."

Kate bit her lip, because she could see herself that Mrs. Lammas might think Andrew was being heartlessly treated, and she was impulsive. "Oh dear," Kate sighed. "And it's stupid because I'm sure she'd really rather have Gail Gowerie for Andrew, and Gail's been to see him every day, and she's surely a lot more suitable for him than I could ever be."

"I couldn't agree more," said Connor cynically. "I hear that he's showing no improvement."

He still thought Kate was afraid of being 'saddled with a cripple,' and she could protest all she liked he would go on believing it. She said, "It's only a week, he *will* get better."

"Let's hope so. And now you're off duty for the week-end?"

All right, he was paying her a wage, but there was no need to sound as though she was clocking off from a job of work. It had been dreadful to see Andrew in that wheel-chair, to push him around from room to room, day following day with no good report.

"Until Sunday evening," she said stonily.

"You'll come back, of course?"

"Of course." She wanted fiercely to pierce his assurance, and she taunted, "But suppose I don't? Suppose I've gone when whoever you send comes to collect me, what could you do about that?"

His eyes narrowed and he said softly, "Look for you myself, Miss Howard, until I found you."

He was most formidable when he was very quiet and she believed that he would hunt for her; and again came the strange terrifying conviction that the world was not big enough to hide her from Connor Lammas.

CHAPTER FOUR

NOTHING had changed in the flat. They talked and talked on Friday evening. On Saturday Kate went into town with Janice, who was buying the week's supplies from the usual supermarket. They kept clear of L and L—once Kate went in there she could have been stuck for hours—and that evening they had a few friends round for supper. On Sunday morning Kate strolled to the park and fed the ducks, just for the pleasure of being able to come and go as she chose. Sunday afternoon she washed and set Susan's hair and her own, and Sunday evening she was in the Range Rover again, being driven back to Lammas Knowle by Elsa's husband, Jack, who was the chauffeur.

Andrew had phoned her this morning while she was out and she'd called him back as soon as she returned. "Where were you?" he had demanded.

"Walking in the park," she'd said. "Feeding the ducks."

"Who was with you?"

"Nobody." Nobody had been, but Andrew gave a disbelieving snort, and when Kate asked,

"How are you?" he'd sounded aggrieved.

"I'm not walking in the park, nor anywhere else. You are coming back this afternoon, aren't you?"

"This evening," she'd said.

When she got back she had to tell him everything she had done, and although it couldn't have been more innocent or more ordinary Andrew acted as though she had had a wild old time. There had been visitors there when Kate first got back. After they left Andrew went to bed, and the nurse left him alone with his mother and with Kate, and Kate's interrogation began.

She answered his questions calmly, but coolly as they be-

...ame more probing, and by the time Andrew was accusing her of heartlessly enjoying herself without a thought for him it was so reminiscent of her mother that Kate could have wept. She wanted to close her ears and draw away, and she said, "Please don't talk like that."

"I missed you," said Andrew sulkily.

"I'm sorry, but I can't stand this third degree. It—it stifles me." She could feel the walls closing in on her and she said abruptly, "I'll see you in the morning," and left the room. Andrew called,

"Kate, come back here!" Mrs. Lammas followed her, and Kate apologised to her too.

"I'm sorry."

Jennifer Lammas looked sympathetic, whispering, although Andrew couldn't have heard normal voices through the thick door. "The poor boy gets so bored, but it will be all right soon, he'll soon be walking again." She squeezed Kate's hand and promised, "We'll go shopping tomorrow and buy some pretty things," so anxious to placate that Kate had to smile.

Next morning at breakfast Connor was told, "Kate and I are going shopping today."

"Are you?"

He glanced across at Kate, with the ironic expression that riled her so much that her knuckles gleamed white as she cut a piece of toast in half, and the knife went through so briskly that she almost cracked the plate.

Jennifer Lammas chattered happily, refilling her own coffee cup, "We'll have a fashion parade this evening and you and Andrew can tell us how nice we look."

Kate went cold at that thought, and Connor said drily, "Fashion parades aren't much in my line, but I'm sure you'll have a rewarding day."

One of the perks of getting into my mother's good books, he meant, collecting the loot; and Kate sat mute and mutinous, more determined than ever to come back from this shopping trip with nothing she hadn't paid for herself.

Jennifer Lammas wouldn't accept it at first. They were set down outside a highly exclusive shop, where she had a 'little account' and where every garment carried an internationally known name, and Kate said, "I shall enjoy going in here and seeing you buy some clothes, but not for me, please, not for me."

"Oh, but you'll find something that's perfect for you, I'm sure you will." Jennifer Lammas was almost at the door, but Kate held her back.

"No," said Kate. "I want to buy my own dress, and it can't be from a place like this. I'm not ungrateful, honestly, it's very kind of you, but please let me keep a little bit of independence." She hated being petty and if it hadn't been for Connor she would have accepted something, not too exorbitantly priced, as a gift from Mrs. Lammas. As it was she sounded desperate, and as Jennifer Lammas protested that this was nonsense she could only mumble miserably, "I suppose it is, but please, I can't take anything, and please don't be offended."

"What a quaint girl you are!" Of course Jennifer Lammas was offended, and cheated too because she had planned to provide Kate with some beautiful clothes so that she could have stood out in any company. It wouldn't have been difficult because Kate was really quite a striking girl, but too modern, too independent. Men didn't like that, Andrew wouldn't, once the novelty had worn off. Andrew expected his world to revolve around him, and Jennifer Lammas was worried again. She said sadly, "Well, now we're here, I suppose I might as well get something for myself."

She was a valued customer. The staff knew what was likely to meet her requirements and brought out several garments, all of which she tried on, buying a dress and a suit. They did their best to tempt Kate, and Kate was sorely tempted. There was one dress that would have cost a month's

...y, and if she had had a month's salary to hand she might have bought it, and if Mrs. Lammas hadn't been Connor Lammas's mother Kate might have borrowed the money from her. But she resolutely remembered Connor, and kept shaking her head and saying no, thank you.

The day didn't turn out badly, though. Kate got a dress, and Jennifer Lammas, looking a little out of place in her real mink coat in a communal changing room, admitted that it looked very nice. It did, although Kate had collected it from the Reductions rail. There were women of all shapes and sizes in here, wriggling in and out of all kinds of clothes. A young woman who was trying on an identical dress looked at Kate and said wistfully, "You can wear anything with your figure, I wish this looked half as good on me," and Jennifer Lammas realised that Kate, with her slender height, her long legs and her gangling grace, did have a natural effortless elegance.

She said warmly, "It's very pretty, dear. Yes, I really think it suits you, and I think I like the green best."

Moira was electric-polishing the floor of the long gallery, when Kate got back to Lammas Knowle and walked into the gallery on her way to her bedroom. Moira waited until Kate was near, then switched off the polisher and asked, "What did you get?"

In front of the family and the rest of the staff—especially Mrs. Shale—Kate could hardly get a word out of Moira. But when they were alone Moira's restraint vanished and the girls chatted on equal terms.

"I'll show you," Kate offered now, and Moira fell into step beside her, goggling at the bag Kate was carrying.

"I thought she was taking you to Germaine's," said Moira.

"She did," said Kate. "Then I took her to C & A."

"Oh!" Moira was disappointed. The staff had presumed that Mrs. Lammas and Kate were shopping for a trousseau.

and Moira had expected Kate to return loaded with beautiful things. This was a nice enough dress. When she reached her room Kate took it out of the bag, and held it up, and Moira could see it would be very attractive when Kate was wearing it. But it didn't look like the start of Mrs. Andrew Lammas's trousseau. She blurted, "This isn't for your trousseau?"

"What? *No!*" Kate almost dropped the dress. She sounded as though she wanted nothing to do with a trousseau, and Moira said,

"You won't be getting married yet, then?" They hadn't discussed Kate's marriage plans, although Kate knew about Moira's young man, a farmer's son living just the other side of Moorton Fells. Since Kate had restyled Moira's hair out of its elastic band and into a prettier style Moira felt that Peter was that much nearer proposing.

"No," said Kate, again with emphasis, and Moira said that it was a smashing dress, and she had better get back to her polishing or Mrs. Shale would slay her.

Connor wasn't home to dinner and Andrew, who didn't seem to mind so much Kate being out with his mother, sat at table with them listening to Mrs. Lammas's account of their day. "We're going to dress up for you later," said Jennifer Lammas, as though that would be a real treat, and Andrew smiled across at Kate,

"What kind of dress is it?"

"A long dress," said Kate.

"A party dress? A dance dress?" He stopped smiling, put down his fork and sat looking mournfully ahead. "I don't suppose I'll ever dance again," he sighed. His mother gave a little cry of distress, but Kate refused to pander to his self-pity.

"Of course you will," she said briskly. "I remember you once telling me that you were bored because everything came too easily. Well, here's a real challenge for you, so

89

e how you face up to it," and for a moment Andrew ked as though he hated her, before he said pettishly,

"Don't bother about my feelings, will you?" He sat through the rest of the meal in sulky silence, and after the meal Kate was despatched by Mrs. Lammas to put on her new dress.

It seemed a waste of time, dressing up to entertain Andrew in his present state of mind, but Mrs. Lammas was changing into her new suit in her room, so Kate put on the green dress, and brushed her hair, then walked back along the corridors and the gallery, down the great staircase, through the hall.

Mrs. Lammas was back already and Nurse Phillips was going into raptures over her suit, the style, the cut and the colour. Both women were being extra bright to coax Andrew out of his sulks, and when Kate walked into the room the nurse clapped her hands. "Oh yes," she said. "Oh, isn't that a little dream of a dress?"

"Marvellous," said Andrew in a flat voice. "It looks very exclusive."

"Funny you should say that," Kate grinned. "There was a row of them in all colours. I couldn't make up my mind between green and yellow until your mother tipped the green."

"You need a necklace with it." Jennifer Lammas went hurrying out of the room, to return carrying a flat leather case, and smiling so that she looked very young and gay. "A necklace like this." She opened the case with a flourish, and on black velvet lay the emeralds she had worn at the dinner party. Kate laughed and gestured them away,

"The dress couldn't live up to them, and I know I couldn't."

"Oh," Nurse Phillips breathed, awestruck, "are they real?"

"I should hope so," said Andrew caustically, and she looked embarrassed.

"Of course they are, how silly of me. Oh, aren't they gorgeous?"

Kate agreed wholeheartedly with that. When Mrs. Lammas took them out of the case they caught the light and blazed like green fire; and when she went to fasten them around Kate's throat Kate stood still, because there were few women alive who wouldn't enjoy wearing that necklace, even if it was only for a couple of minutes.

"A perfect match," Jennifer Lammas said merrily, and Andrew smiled, and Nurse Phillips clapped again, and Kate went to look at herself in one of the pair of Louis Quinze mirrors that hung each side one of the windows. She gulped at her reflection. Goodness knows what this necklace was worth, the emeralds were perfectly graded, each stone set in diamonds. Then her lips twitched as she wondered what Sue and Janice would say if they could see her, in a dress from the Reductions rail and a matching necklace that happened to be worth a fortune.

"They suit you," said Jennifer Lammas. "Don't they, Andrew? Don't they, Nurse?" And probably Andrew and the nurse agreed, all in the spirit of the game, but as that was the moment Connor Lammas opened the door Kate didn't hear what they said.

He saw her before he saw anyone else. In her bright green dress, and the emeralds, she was the most conspicuous figure in the room, and when his mother went to meet him he still kept his eyes on Kate. "Hello, dear," said his mother. "Have you had a hard day?"

He was looking grim, but he said, "Not particularly. What's going on here?"

"I told you this morning—Kate and I have been shopping."

"Miss Howard seems to have done well," said Connor, and Jennifer Lammas laughed.

"They match her dress, don't they?"

91

"Admirably," he said. "But it's a little premature to deck her out in the family heirlooms."

Kate was already fumbling with the fastener, and Nurse Phillips said, "Good evening, Mr. Lammas, if you'll excuse me," and retreated hastily. If he was annoyed that his mother had let Kate wear the emeralds Nurse Phillips wanted no part of the scene. She didn't fancy getting on the wrong side of Connor Lammas.

It was a complicated clasp and Kate looked appealingly at Mrs. Lammas, who came to her aid and said reproachfully, "That wasn't a very nice thing to say, Connor."

"I apologise. They do indeed match the dress." The steel-grey eyes summed up the picture Kate made, and the inquiry was double-edged. "Do you propose lending them to Miss Howard?"

He sounded as though Kate would almost certainly decamp with the emeralds or switch them for counterfeits, and she smiled brilliantly at Mrs. Lammas and said in a high-pitched voice, "Thank you, that was fun." Then she turned on Connor, her voice still too high but the smile wiped clean from her face. "When I want green beads to wear with my dress," she said with biting precision, "I'll buy some glass ones. Or they do some very pretty lines in plastic these days. Peasants like myself can't tell them from the real thing."

Mrs. Lammas squeezed Kate's arm pleadingly. "Kate, please don't be angry, and Connor, I don't think Kate would wear my jewellery if I did offer to lend it to her. She doesn't accept favours, she wouldn't let me buy her so much as a scarf today." Her face puckered. "She bought one dress, that one, herself, and I was very disappointed."

"I could have told you that Kate accepts nothing," said Andrew smugly. "She's terrified of being beholden. You won't catch Kate with the usual bait." He had tried expensive gifts when he first met her and they had got him nowhere, but now he sounded triumphant, and Kate said,

"I'll go and change." Mrs. Lammas still held the emeralds dangling from her fingers. "And you'd better lock those away," said Kate, and almost ran from the room.

The first time she came here Connor had seen her looking at the emeralds and believed she was yearning for them. Now tonight she was wearing them, and although they seemed to be entailed to Connor he probably thought she hoped that Mrs. Lammas would let her borrow them. And Mrs. Lammas might have done, the girl she saw as Andrew's future wife. No, thank you, thought Kate, I'd be terrified the clasp would come undone, or I'd look down and find the biggest stone had dropped out of its setting; and my flesh would crawl wearing Connor Lammas's property.

In the gallery she passed the portrait of the Georgian lady wearing the emeralds, and gave her a wry smile. Leonora Lammas looked content with her lot, and she was beautifully painted. I must start painting again, Kate thought. I could be here for some time yet, but it need not be time wasted.

She lingered over changing her dress. She was loath to go back to Connor, but she didn't want him to think his insults had shattered her so that she couldn't face him. Eventually she left her bedroom, and she took a sketch pad and pencils with her.

Connor wasn't in the drawing room. Nurse Phillips had returned, she and Mrs. Lammas were watching television. Andrew seemed to be watching the door. He was facing it, and as Kate walked in he said, "You took your time."

"Sorry," said Kate. She took a chair, and balanced her sketch pad on her knee.

"What are you doing?" Andrew asked.

"Making some sketches."

"What for?"

"To amuse myself."

"You find the company dull?" said Andrew, and his

93

mother cast him an imploring glance, after which he watched the television screen too, and Kate went on with her sketching.

She made sketches of the three of them on one page: Andrew, handsomely sulky; Jennifer Lammas with the exquisite bone structure of face that would last longer than life; and Nurse Phillips. She spent longest on Nurse Phillips, putting the gleam of humour in her eyes and getting across the basic kindness. When she sat back, her pencil idle, Andrew asked, "May I see?" and Kate took the sketch pad to him.

The two women got up and leaned over as Andrew held the pad, and there was a chorus of delight from them—from the women, not from Andrew. Kate had worked off her exasperation portraying him vividly and moodily. He looked very bad-tempered, and now he tore off the page and ripped it across and across. "Thank you," he said. "How would you look if you were in my state? There isn't much to laugh at."

"I'm sorry," Kate said again. She always seemed to be having to apologise to Andrew, and his mother said hastily, "They were very good, Kate, you're very clever."

Nurse Phillips was on her knees, picking up the torn pieces and looking as distressed as though something of real value had been spoiled. Her sketch had been ripped beyond repair and she said dolefully, "I'd have liked that for my mother, she'd have liked it."

"I'll do another," Kate offered. "I'll do it right now."

"Would you?" Nurse Phillips coloured with pleasure. "That would be really very kind of you."

"And you can do me again," said Andrew. "I could be the perfect sitter. I can't walk away."

Kate had once thought she would like to paint Andrew, he was one of the best looking men she had ever met, and both Andrew and his mother were enthusiastic about the idea. That evening she finished the sketch for Nurse Phillips, and next day she began to make preliminary sketches of Andrew. All the equipment she needed—canvas, easel, brushes, palette and paints—would be arriving, and Kate worked happily, trying to decide the form of the portrait.

Gail looked in, as usual, this time during the afternoon. They were in the library, Kate was using the big table, immersed in the effort of catching Andrew's changing expressions. Gail was trying to persuade him to let her drive him round to visit friends next day, but she wasn't succeeding; and when Andrew was wheeled away for his therapy treatment Gail sat on the edge of the table, swinging a leg and looking disconsolate.

"His friends will just have to go on coming here, won't they?" she sighed. "Although the doctor said it would be all right for him to go in the car. The doctor said it was a good idea."

She had told Andrew that and got the mulish look that Kate was trying to avoid in this portrait, although goodness knows it was typical of Andrew. Gail pointed to one of the sketches and said, "That's good. That's beautiful."

"He is beautiful," said Kate.

Gail looked at the other sketches, Kate's day's work. "He always was," she said. "I've known him all my life. We've always been together a lot, I suppose that's why the mamas thought we'd make a match of it."

"Did you think that?" Kate went on with her sketching prepared for Gail to clam up, although it was Gail who had provided an opening for the question.

But Gail said bluntly, "You mean, am I in love with him?"

"Are you?"

Gail did pick up a sketch then, a full-face that captured Andrew's little-boy-lost look, and almost seemed to be talking to it. "Since the accident I've realised I'd have hated him to have killed himself. He's rather a dear when he isn't

95

being stupid, like trying to jump Halla or getting mixed up
—" She stuck there, and Kate laughed and finished it for
her.

"Getting mixed up with unsuitable girls?"

"You're different," Gail admitted rather grudgingly. "But
the one before you cost a bomb."

"Who paid, Andrew or Connor?" Kate put aside the
sketch she had been doing, and started another, from memory
and with malice.

"Andrew most of the time," said Gail. "She was a folk
singer, and Andrew showered money on that group like
pennies from heaven, although anyone with eyes could see
how it was between her and the lead guitar. Connor put his
foot down in the end, and I think he paid her off."

"I thought he'd had practice in paying off," muttered
Kate. She was making a sketch of Connor now, and she wondered why she hadn't done it before because it was very
satisfying.

"The one before that," said Gail with an understandable
lack of sympathy, "had her sights on Connor, not Andrew.
She was an American, and she led Andrew on and he
thought she was sensational." Gail rolled her big blue eyes.
"And she was. So darn glamorous that it couldn't be true.
When she couldn't get Connor she went back home and
married somebody who was in oil." From Gail's expression
he was up to his neck in it, and Kate couldn't hold back the
giggles. Gail was relating Andrew's misfortunes with a relish
that showed they had been balm to her wounded pride.

"If she was so glamorous," Kate was sketching again now,
her pencil moving quickly and surely, "why wasn't she good
enough for Connor?"

"Connor makes his own selection." Gail shrugged. "And
perhaps he thought she'd expect too much of his time and
attention. He's got all the charm in the world when he
chooses to use it," Kate's sniff went unnoticed, "but there's

precious little sentiment in him. He'd never lose his head over anything, certainly not over a woman."

"A man of stone?" Kate suggested, and Gail smiled slowly.

"Right through," she agreed.

"Portrait of a man of stone," said Kate. She held up her sketch. At first glance it was an Easter Island head, one of those gigantic identical figures from pre-history, whose long heavy-lidded faces stare up at the skies or across the Pacific Ocean. But at second glance it was Connor Lammas, his mouth, his eyes, his arrogant look.

Gail yelped, recognising it, "*Connor*!"

"Thank you," said Kate.

"It's him all right, but it isn't very flattering." Gail had her hand over her mouth, as though laughter might be out of place. "You're not going to show it him?"

"You don't think he'd appreciate it?" Kate pretended to be serious and Gail was saying, "Well, it is a caricature, I don't think I'd like you to caricature me," when she realised that Kate was smiling.

Kate dropped the sketch into her portfolio, and the portfolio into a drawer, and said, "Connor disapproves of me enough as it is, I'm not going out of my way to annoy him."

"That would be silly," Gail looked down again at the sketches of Andrew, her round face pensive, "when it's beginning to look as though Andrew might have found the right girl in you."

Kate said nothing, but her expression spoke volumes, and Gail was less surprised than she might have been. She was a close observer of Kate and Andrew, and although Kate seemed as concerned about Andrew as anyone could be there was no possessiveness in her. She kept in the background, didn't compete with his visitors, not even with Gail, and that wasn't because she was shy.

Gail had been wondering if seeing Andrew as a peevish

invalid had cooled Kate's affections. If it had she couldn't have cared much in the first place, the poor love really did seem to be jinxed in the girls he picked, and perhaps this might shake some sense into him. Gail hadn't quite made up her mind what her own feelings were, but she was pleased by Kate's unspoken admission that she was no rival.

Gail decided to stay for dinner, so dinner was a lively meal because she was as compulsive a chatterer as Mrs. Lammas. Connor, who ate with them, was told that Kate had been sketching Andrew all day, Gail went into transports about Kate's skill, and Kate protested, "You're exaggerating wildly."

"Well, I think *every* sketch was really something." Gail slipped Kate a sly grin, and Kate knew they were sharing a joke at Connor's expense, and Gail was feeling very daring. Gail looked at Connor, and away quickly, and seemed about to dissolve into giggles until Andrew asked suspiciously,

"What was funny about them? Unless there were some I didn't see."

He had been put out last night when Kate portrayed him looking sulky and, while she was reassuring him that he had inspected every sketch she had made of him today, she was wondering how Connor would react if he saw himself as an Easter Island image. He would probably go into the library to look at the sketches now there had been talk about them, and it was possible he might open the drawer and find the portfolio. It was just possible, and Kate would be safer with that sketch destroyed. It wouldn't really matter if Connor saw it, but better not.

When the meal was over Connor went, and as soon as she could, without obviously going in hot pursuit, Kate dashed down to the library. He was in there, standing at the table, looking at the sketches, and when she walked in he seemed as though he had expected her. He said, "They were right. You do have promise."

"Thank you. Who was right, apart from Gail?" She walked round the table so that she was in front of the drawer where she had slipped the portfolio.

"Angus Morrison and Felix Klopper." He held one of the sketches. His nails were square and immaculately manicured, but it was a hand that could grip like a vice and he had boxer's shoulders beneath that jacket. A powerful man in every way. "Why don't you submit some pictures to Klopper?" he asked.

"For your gallery?" This was an offer she hadn't expected, and he put down the sketch and looked at her.

"I've a financial interest, but Felix runs the Klopper Galleries and he lowers his standards for nobody. You'd be getting no favours."

When she worked in St. Ives she had painted pictures that had been displayed in one of the shops, and tourists had bought them. She had painted during her brief stay in that artists' commune, and left the paintings behind when she left. She didn't really know whether her standard was high or low, but this was a chance of an expert's opinion.

"Thank you," she said, and wondered if Connor Lammas was expecting Felix Klopper to report that her gift was uninspired. She must be prepared for disappointment, she mustn't let Connor Lammas get under her guard. He'd never let her get under his, and a sudden spirit of mischief seized her.

She opened the drawer and took the sketch from the portfolio and laid it on the table before him. "Something else I did today," she said. She had known he wouldn't be oversensitive, as Andrew was to any suggestion of criticism. Nor had she expected anger for such a small matter, just a wry admission that she had scored a hit with this unflattering likeness. What she was unprepared for was that he should chuckle and then roar with laughter, and she began to smile herself although her eyes were puzzled. It seemed there were times when Connor Lammas did not take himself seriously.

"Portrait of a man of stone," she said. "Right through, according to Gail."

He raised an eyebrow, still laughing. "And how would she know?"

She floundered, "Hasn't she had—all her life to observe you?"

"Appearances can be deceptive." That was a cliché but it was true, and she gasped,

"You wouldn't be saying you're really soft-centred?"

"Hardly." As he said—hardly. But if he wasn't talking about himself what was he talking about?

"Not *me*?" She jabbed herself with a fingertip, because that was almost equally surprising. "Is it possible you're wondering if you were wrong about *me*?"

"It's possible," he said. "You're excessively independent, and you're talented enough to make your own way, so why should your goal in life be a rich husband?"

"It isn't," she said. "When Andrew walks again I shall tell him again that it isn't."

"But not until he walks," said Connor, and this time it was a request, although she couldn't have refused.

"Of course not," she said.

"Thank you."

"Could I—go out on the moors to paint?" She was having difficulty with her voice, it was catching in her throat. "Andrew doesn't like me to leave the grounds, but he doesn't really need me all the time."

"Of course you can leave the grounds. You're not a prisoner here."

"I've felt like one. If I could just walk out and not have to say where I've been."

"Is is that bad?" She nodded. "I'll talk to him," said Connor.

"Please." She offered him the sketch. "Do you want this?"

100

and he asked,

"How much? As a professional you shouldn't give your work away."

"It only took me a few minutes." She tried to smile. "Or are you excessively independent too?"

"Yes, I suppose I am." He spoke slowly. "We seem to have something in common." And again they were facing each other like duellers, with that unblinking awareness, but this time there was something else, a searching.

What am I looking for? Kate thought wildly. Why is he looking at me like that? It was only a few seconds before Connor took the sketch and said, "Thank you," and Kate said,

"I must get back," and moved quickly away. Her heart was racing. He had always done that to her. It was one of the things she resented about him, that he broke down her barriers of reserve. She had had every reason to dislike him, and he had had cause to distrust her—Andrew's choice of girl-friends had been pretty abysmal, and Kate's record hadn't seem to promise much improvement.

But Connor had just admitted he had been wrong in assuming she was after Andrew's money, so was this a truce? And what would take the place of hostility if they ceased to be enemies? Not indifference. She couldn't imagine feeling nothing when Connor was near. She was aware of him in every nerve and that wasn't going to change, or her heart wouldn't be beating like this now. But, if he wasn't her enemy, then what was he to her that no man had ever been before?

Gail stayed on, and during the evening other friends called, and Kate had to bring up the sketches of Andrew for them to examine. Connor hadn't appeared again, she supposed he was working in the study, and as she gathered up the sketches from the library table she looked at the connecting door and wished it would open and Connor would say, "Come and talk to me, because I'm in utter confusion about you."

That was very unlikely. He might not be in the study, he didn't know she was here, and he had probably not given her another thought. But Kate was confused. She would have liked to slip away alone, over to the island, but it was night time now and she had to take back the sketches to the drawing room where they were waiting for her.

The sketches were admired all round. Mrs. Lammas was still gloating over them when the visitors left. She knew that Kate had worked as a commercial artist in L and L, and she had thought the sketches last night were good, but it was delightful to have these enchanting studies of Andrew. She simply couldn't make up her mind how she would like him to be painted, full face or profile or three-quarter face.

She was full of praise for Kate. There were plenty of paintings of bygone Lammases in Lammas Knowle, but none of her sons, and she said, "When you've finished Andrew's portrait, my dear, I suppose you wouldn't let me try to persuade Connor to sit for you?"

Andrew said, "Don't be ridiculous, Mother, can you see Connor agreeing to spend his time sitting for a portrait? And if he did he'd want an R.A., not Kate," and Mrs. Lammas sighed and agreed.

Kate agreed too; she didn't want to paint Connor. It had been easy enough making a caricature of him, but she could never paint his portrait. She would probably get the shakes so badly she wouldn't be able to hold the brush.

"How long should the painting take?" Mrs. Lammas asked.

"About a week," said Kate. "Connor said anything I did afterwards I could submit to the Klopper Galleries."

"No hurry with the portrait," said Andrew with his martyred air, "I've got all the time in the world."

"If you mean in that chair," said Kate quietly, "that isn't what the doctors say. Not unless that's how you want it. It is up to you."

Andrew's face went white. "I can't move," he said. "Can't you understand that? Ever since you got me to ride that damned horse I haven't been able to move. I'm a cripple!" He was almost shouting, gripping the arms of his wheelchair, and Nurse Phillips, who had been sitting in a corner with a book, came over and said,

"Bedtime, I think."

"Stop treating me like a child!" Andrew snarled at her.

"Then stop acting like one," Nurse Phillips retorted reasonably. "It's right what Miss Howard says, you have got to help yourself."

"Some of us are able to do that easier than others," said Andrew. "If Connor had been thrown he'd have been on his feet by now, wouldn't he?"

"He probably would," sighed their mother, and Andrew practically screamed at her,

"But I am not Connor, and I cannot *move*!" He was working himself into near-hysteria, and the nurse looked as though she longed to tell her fractious patient a few more home truths, or failing that, shake him. But Mrs. Lammas was in tears, and with her heart condition this was bad for her.

"Fetch Connor, Kate," Mrs. Lammas quavered, and Kate ran to the study. Of course Connor could have been anywhere, out of the house altogether, but the study seemed a likely place, and he answered her knock on the door as she opened the door.

She gasped, "I'm sorry, but will you come, please? Andrew's upset and it's not doing your mother any good." Connor was beside her, before she'd finished explaining, asking,

"What's upset him?"

"I'm afraid I did, I told him it was up to him how soon

he walked again."

"He's been told that before."

"Well, he didn't want to hear it tonight. It is true, isn't it?"

"Quite true." She was almost trotting to keep pace with Connor's stride, and when they reached the drawing room Nurse Phillips was bending over Mrs. Lammas who had obviously just swallowed a couple of her pills.

"All right?" Connor went to his mother, and she reached out a groping hand for him, smiling weakly, echoing,

"All right."

He looked across at Andrew, whose face was puckered like a small boy's. "Why won't anyone believe me?" Andrew was wailing. "I *can't* move my legs. There's no feeling in them. God knows I'd walk if I could."

His mother's eyes were still brimming with tears and Connor said, "Kate, would you take her to bed?" The nurse nodded silent agreement, and Kate put an arm round Mrs. Lammas and got her out of the room. They went slowly, and as soon as the door was closed Jennifer Lammas breathed a deep sigh and made a fair job of pulling herself together. She said, "He's going to be all right, of course, but it is heartbreaking to see him so frightened and so weak."

"I know," Kate soothed her. "But try not to let it upset you. Keep remembering that he will be well again."

She stayed to see Jennifer Lammas in bed, the colour back in her cheeks and looking set for a restful night. Jennifer Lammas kissed her and said, "Goodnight, Kate, thank you," and then, "Did you notice just now, for the first time Connor called you Kate?"

"I noticed," Kate smiled, "but he was rather preoccupied. wasn't he?"

Jennifer Lammas was smiling too. "It's a beginning. You two will be friends yet."

As Kate walked down empty corridors, past closed doors, she thought—this is no beginning. It's the first time he has called me Kate, but I've struggled against his hands, broken away and still felt his touch on my skin. He called me Kate, but what do I call him?

She could have gone to her own room. Today had been long enough and she already had enough on her mind to keep her awake, but she felt that she should go downstairs and tell Connor that Mrs. Lammas was all right now, and ask how Andrew was. So she went downstairs, back to the drawing room, where the door was open and Connor was sitting alone, smoking a cigar. He got up as she entered the room.

"She's in bed," she said. "I think she'll sleep."

"Good. Will you join me?" On a table, by the chair on which he had been sitting, were a couple of decanters on a silver tray, whisky and brandy. He had been drinking brandy and Kate said,

"Not for me, thanks." Her head was muzzy enough tonight, but she didn't want to go and she changed her mind almost before the words were out. "A very small one, then." At the first splash of brandy she said, "That's enough," and he handed it to her with a half smile.

"I wasn't trying to get you drunk."

"I didn't think you were," she said, feeling gauche, sitting holding her glass.

"In any case I'm sure you have a cool head."

They were not sniping at each other now, and she could see what Gail meant when she'd said Connor had all the charm in the world when he chose to use it. She began to relax, her stiff lips softening and curving.

"But no match for yours," she said, and they smiled at each other. One gulp and her glass would be empty, so she just went on holding it, and Connor drew on his cigar and she asked, "Did you convince Andrew he'll get back the use of his legs?"

"He knows that, although he might begin to doubt it if you walked out on him." When Connor's voice was not biting it was deep and slow and rather attractive. The face was uncompromising, full of character. It would take a long time to know this man. You could never know him unless he wanted you to, and of course he didn't. He was as unlikely to open his heart to Kate as he was to open his arms, and she felt colour rising in her face at the unthinkable thought of herself in Connor's embrace, held with a passion that was not anger.

She put down her glass by her feet, needing her hands to hide her hot cheeks, giving all her attention to what he was saying about Andrew.

"I think I've persuaded him that the melodrama must stop. Mainly because it puts an unnecessary strain on my mother. Otherwise I'd have asked you and the nurse to overlook it—Andrew enjoys self-dramatisation."

Kate was coming to realise that. She asked wryly, "Is that why his choice runs to pricey, very unsuitable girl-friends?"

"You've heard about them?" Connor's cynical expression had no sting in it because he wasn't including her, and she could smile as she nodded and said,

"And you thought I was carrying on the tradition?"

"It looked that way."

"But appearances—"

He finished it, "—can be deceptive." After a moment he asked, "What did happen? How did you get involved?"

He was ready to listen to her version now, and she told him eagerly, "You probably know I bumped into Andrew in the corridor at work, he knocked a coffee tray out of my hands. That was an accident, I certainly wasn't engineering anything, but that evening it was raining and he offered me a lift and invited himself in for a coffee."

To tell her he was bored with his work, he wanted to be

a writer. Perhaps while she was doing her painting Andrew might start to write something. Although goodness knows what, and if he had had any real writer's urge he would surely have produced something long ago.

She shrugged, because from now on there wasn't much to tell. "We went out together, often with friends, my other friends. That's how I thought of Andrew, as another friend."

"Did he ask you to marry him?"

"Well, yes, he did, but he knew I didn't want to marry him, that I didn't want to marry anyone." She picked up her glass again, with its minute quantity of brandy. "I suppose that was my main attraction," she decided. "He always seems to pick the ones who—" Who don't want him sounded unkind, although the previous two had preferred other men. She said, "Who would be hard to get," and Connor agreed grimly,

"It is becoming a repeating pattern."

"Will you go on—er—bailing him out indefinitely?"

"No. But if he makes a destructive marriage my mother will take it badly. She suffers with Andrew. They're alike in many ways."

She knew that too, but Kate was grateful for the confidence, as a gesture of trust, and she asked, "Who are you like? your father?" remembering the big handsome jolly-looking man in the photographs.

Connor smiled. "Not particularly, I'm probably a throwback. What about you?"

Kate had looked like neither of her parents, she had been like neither of them. Her smile was forced. "Another throwback," she said.

"Something else we have in common." He looked at her again with that searching look, and she dared not breathe, she dared not move. It was as though she was hiding and must make no sound or she would be found.

When she forced herself to speak it was a tremendous effort, she could hardly believe that her voice would sound so normal. "There can't be much more." He was a millionaire and she was poor as a church mouse. There couldn't be much they had in common, but he said quietly,

"You think not?" and then, "I'm grateful for what you're doing, I apologise for my previous attitude."

"It was understandable," she said, "and it's forgotten."

"Thank you." He had finished his drink and she swallowed hers, feeling it burn and tickle the back of her throat, and stood up.

"I have to start painting a portrait tomorrow," she said.

Connor opened the door for her into the great hall. She didn't reach to turn the knob this time so she didn't brush his hand, but she wondered if he remembered what he had said when she'd flinched from him.

She remembered. "It's forgotten," she'd said just now, but she wasn't going to find it easy to forget anything about Connor Lammas, enemy, friend, whatever he was.

She stepped out into the hall, passing him, the tall figure in the dark well-cut suit. "Goodnight," she said.

"Goodnight, Kate." She looked back as he spoke because he sounded as though he had more to say, and he looked down at her, almost scowling, dark brows drawn together. Then he turned abruptly back into the drawing room and closed the door.

Connor had read Andrew the riot act so that, although Andrew was still sorry for himself and everyone was sorry for him, he said no more in front of his mother about being permanently crippled. But he said nothing about walking either, and that week passed with no discernible improvement.

It was on Connor's orders that Mrs. Yeomans arrived with a folder full of office work. Andrew had declined to go into the store, he was refusing to go anywhere, unwilling to see any but close friends. But Mrs. Yeomans had been Andrew's personal secretary and assistant for the four years he had been general manager, and she managed to involve him again in the administration of the store.

It was an occupation for his mind, and he needed one. He wasn't going to write a book. When Kate suggested he might he looked at her blankly. "You told me you always wanted to be a writer," she said.

"So I do," said Andrew, "and some time I will."

This year, next year, some time, never, Kate was sure. She went on with the portrait she was painting of him, while everyone tried to keep him happy.

Connor was away from Wednesday. Kate saw him briefly at breakfast, but after that he wasn't home. She missed him, which was surprising, but now they had called a truce she was intrigued by him. He was ruthless, hard, too self-sufficient, too strong, but interesting. At odd moments of the day—and night—she found herself thinking about Connor. It wasn't really personal, of course, it was because he intrigued her as a complex personality.

After lunch on Wednesday she said, "I'd like to go for a walk," and Andrew said bitterly,

"So would I."

"I mean, I'd like to go out on the moors." She had worded that tactlessly, she might have known how Andrew would react. Now he said sarcastically,

"Connor's orders, you're to go and come as you like, so can I ask if you'll be back today?"

Gail and Mrs. Lammas were there; Kate had spent the morning on the portrait and she would be back before Andrew was through his physiotherapy session. She said, "I won't be long," and Gail laughed, a brittle sound like crackling ice.

"I'm here, or hadn't you noticed? If Kate wants to go

109

for a walk it doesn't mean you're being abandoned by the human race."

"Good old Gail," said Andrew, and he did seem rather ashamed of himself.

"I don't know why I bother," snapped Gail. Then she started to laugh again, real laughter this time. "Except that you did visit me every day when I had chickenpox." That seemed to be an old joke. Andrew smiled, and Mrs. Lammas joined in the laughter as Kate slipped out of the room.

As a child Kate had escaped sometimes to the moors, running through the ferns and bracken, and this was an escape now. She felt free as a bird loosed from a cage, but she was back in just over an hour, she didn't want to take too much advantage of her concessions.

On Thursday it rained, so on Thursday afternoon she went to the island instead. Friday was overcast, a threatening day, the day on which they were expecting Connor home.

Kate was going home to the flat on Saturday morning this weekend, staying until Sunday night. She had phoned the girls and told them about the portrait, and the paintings she was hoping to do. Janice, who had taken the call, said, "You sound a lot happier."

"I am," Kate admitted. "I'll tell you about it when I see you." She couldn't relate openly, from a phone in Lammas Knowle, that Gail seemed prepared to take Andrew off her hands, nor that she and Connor were now behaving in a civilised fashion towards each other.

Kate was happier, but on Friday she felt restless and unsettled. The weather might have had something to do with that. The sky was so dark it was hard to tell where the clouds ended and the hills began. It was oppressive and disturbing, and Kate was glad of an excuse to put down her brushes when Mrs. Yeomans arrived with work for Andrew.

She went looking for Mrs. Lammas and said, "I'm going for a walk, that will be all right, won't it?"

"It isn't a very nice day, dear." Jennifer Lammas looked apprehensively through the nearest window, but Kate smiled,

"I'll wear a mac, it won't hurt me."

She tied a scarf over her head, but pulled it off before she reached the bridge and let the wind blow through her hair. There was storm all around, in little growls of thunder, as she walked across the main track into the hills. Andrew's portrait was almost done, she had made it a photographic likeness because that was what he and his mother expected, but she wanted to paint out here on the moors. To paint as she felt, to capture a feeling.

She went on walking even when the rain came, crossing tracks but meeting no one, until she came to Merlin's Cut, where Andrew had fallen from Halla. This was two miles from the house. Andrew had ridden the horse so far, and most likely he could have brought himself back safe and sound if he hadn't tried to jump this little barrier of rock. That had been unnecessary bravado, sheer cussedness according to Bert the groom who had followed him.

Halla was still at Lammas Knowle. When he was home Connor still rode him regularly. One day last week Kate and Gail had been wheeling Andrew through the courtyard while Bert was grooming the horse, and Andrew had said, "I'd like to put a bullet through that damned animal's head."

He probably hadn't meant it, but the groom had come across looking very pugnacious and growled, "You were warned, weren't you? Wasn't I shouting myself hoarse at you not to jump him? Didn't you always know there's only one man he trusts?"

Gail had wheeled Andrew away, and Kate had stayed to pacify Bert, because he really loved that horse and he was glaring as though Andrew was planning its execution. Of course Andrew wasn't, but of course he wished he had never ridden Halla, and Kate turned from Merlin's Cut with a sigh.

The rain was drenching by now. Her mac, buttoned up to the neck with collar raised, kept out most of it, but some dripped down her gumboots, and her hair was as wet as the heather. It should have been horrible, but it wasn't, it was exhilarating, and although she knew she should be going back she went on, leaving Merlin's Cut far behind, climbing hills, slithering down, walking across rough open tracts of moorland, skirting rocks, taking stepping stones over the occasional stream.

This was more than a little crazy. By the time she had battled her way back to Lammas Knowle she was going to be exhausted, and she might not find her way back all that easily. Of course she *would* find her way, but she had walked for miles, and each step had to be retraced, so it was crazy to keep walking, putting more distance between herself and Lammas Knowle, when she knew that she was tiring.

But she did keep walking, until at last she had to stop, because her legs and her back were aching and her gumboots weighed a ton. She had to rest for a while, and then she would go back. She sat down on a very damp rock, near the top of a hill where an overhanging formation of rock made a shelter of sorts, and looked back.

There was no sign of life. She was alone with the thunder rolling around the sky, the odd flash of lightning slashing the black clouds, the steady falling rain. If I could paint this, she thought, the loneliness, the terrible beauty, that would be something to show Connor.

She sat watching, resting, not waiting, but when she saw the horse and the man on a faraway hill, it was as though she had been waiting. They came galloping towards her, through the wind and the rain. Halla's coat gleamed like black satin as Connor dismounted at the foot of the hill.

"Are you all right?" Connor called.

"Fine," she called back.

He tethered Halla's bridle to a rock and began to climb the hill towards her, asking, "What are you doing out here on a day like this?"

"I was looking for something to paint." She stood up, but stayed where she was, in her little shelter, and as he reached her he asked,

"How do you intend to get your equipment four miles from the house and back?"

Rain streamed down his face from his hair, and off the heavy mac he wore. She wouldn't have been surprised if he had looked furious, but he didn't.

"I got carried away," she explained. "I just went on walking. I quite like storms."

He smiled at that. "That I believe."

"Anyhow, what are you doing here?"

"Looking for you," he said. "They told me you'd been gone for hours and I had visions of you holed up somewhere with a sprained ankle."

He had come looking for her, for her sake, not Andrew's. He was breathing fast, surely not from climbing the hill, perhaps from the battle against the wind and the rain.

"I'm sorry," she said unsteadily. "I didn't realise anyone would be worried." Andrew perhaps, but not Connor, and Andrew's concern was selfish, but Connor had thought she might need help.

She hardly dared look at him. She was shaking, she was scared. She had walked into the storm because he was coming back today, and she didn't know what was going to happen. She had been running from him again, because she was more afraid of him now that he was not her enemy.

The moors stretched for miles. A helicopter could have flown over them without pinpointing a fugitive. Her white mac made her conspicuous, but he could have had no idea which direction she had taken, and yet—"You found me," she whispered, and he looked down at her.

"Yes," he said, in a voice she did not recognise, "I've found you."

CHAPTER FIVE

KATE started to talk quickly. "How long have you been looking for me? What are the odds against finding someone out here just like that?"

She sounded amused at this odd situation, but she didn't think Connor was fooled. He knew she was shaking. "Halla covers a lot of ground in a very short time," he said.

They stood together under the shelf of rock, and as Kate felt her feet squelch in her gumboots she realised she was tense right down to the ends of her toes. Down below Halla threw back his head, tossing rain from his mane, and Kate said, "You wouldn't be thinking of giving me a lift, would you?"

"Of course." When the steel grey eyes glinted with laughter the hard face was devastatingly attractive.

"I can't ride a horse," she said, "I could fall off a donkey," and when Connor laughed she laughed too. Then she asked, "Why won't he jump with anyone else?"

"He was taking a hedge near the Irish border," Connor told her, "and a landmine went off. His weight must have triggered it, he wasn't on it, but he was close."

"Were you riding him?" Andrew had told her that first day that Halla was bred in Ireland.

"No, and the man who was was lucky. The blast caught them, shook him up; he wasn't hurt, but Halla was shell-shocked. I hadn't bought him then, but I'd seen him and liked him and I was over there to buy a horse." He smiled. "Afterwards he wouldn't let anyone else near him, so that settled it."

It couldn't have been that easy. It must have needed endless patience to win an animal's trust so that, so long as

Connor rode him, he would take what must be every time a leap in the dark. Andrew had known why it was madness to try to jump Halla, so why on earth had he done it? Kate said quietly, "I didn't know. Andrew said you were the only one who could ride Halla, the last man who tried was thrown, but I didn't know why, and when I said, 'Ride that horse of his,' I didn't mean to be taken literally." She gestured helplessly. "I suppose I meant—go away and leave me alone."

Connor raised an eyebrow. "He'd just asked me to marry him," she explained, "by special licence so that when you found out it would be too late to do much about it. He said you wouldn't waste your time making a fuss then."

"That sounds a practical proposal," said Connor drily.

"Would you have made a fuss?" But instead of answering her question Connor asked another.

"If he'd worded that differently might you have considered it?"

"*No*, and he knew it. Unless he thought I was playing hard to get." The wind whipped her hair across her face and she looked at Connor through the tangle. "I seem to have been pretty generally misunderstood by the Lammas family."

"Not by me," said Connor, and when she froze, her hand brushing her hair from her eyes, "not entirely."

"What do you mean?" she asked through lips that felt dry although a mist of rain was on her face.

He wasn't smiling, he was almost frowning. "When you walked into that office," he said, "I thought—my God, not this one. She isn't right for Andrew in any way."

That was true, she knew that. She said, "You worked that out from my dossier?"

"No, I knew that when I saw you." He was looking at her now and he was too close for comfort. She moved a sideways step and was grateful for a faint rumble of thunder and a small flash of lightning, that made Halla lift his

116

head and look for Connor. She said, fast but not quite steadily,

"I was sitting here wishing I could paint this scene with the storm around. Not every cloud, of course, not like I painted Andrew with every detail in, but the wildness and the loneliness. Halla looks like part of it, doesn't he?"

"So do you." Connor reached to touch her hair, lifting it lightly from her face. He was smiling again now, the lines creased at the corner of his eyes, a corner of the mouth lifting in a lopsided grin. "Are you sure your parents weren't gipsies?" he said.

Kate's lips trembled, but she hoped it looked like a smile. "If they were it was generations ago. My parents were not travelling folk."

"Home-lovers?" He spoke very quietly They were so close there was no need to raise voices above a whisper.

"Not that either." Her voice was hardly a whisper, she spoke on a breath. "Although they stayed at home."

He looked at her as though she was telling him everything, as though he knew it all, right back to the beginning. "Not a happy childhood?" he said, and when she shook her head he took her in his arms, pressed against him, damp cheek against wet mac. She closed her eyes and the tension left her, and she could have stayed here for ever, saying nothing, not trying to analyse this strange floating feeling.

She could feel her own heartbeats and she could hear Connor's heart, through shirt, jacket, mac. She was sure she could hear his heart, so he wasn't stone all through, and she raised her face, and tilted her head back to look up at him, and blinked and stammered, "G—goodness!"

He blinked too. The grey eyes were piercing, they were always piercing, but he looked shaken for a moment. Then he said, "As you say—goodness," and slowly they smiled at each other.

"Well now," said Connor.

"It isn't going to stop raining," said Kate. "I think I should be starting to walk back."

"Very well." He loosed her from the circle of his arms and held out a hand. She took the hand, and needed it as they went down the hill because she had already walked for miles, and because she wasn't feeling quite herself, and because her gumboots were heavy.

Halla, only trusting one man, waited for Connor. As Connor untied the rein from the tethering rock Kate stood well to one side. "Are you scared of him?" Connor asked, and she said shrilly,

"Of course I'm scared of him!"

He smiled at her. "What I meant was, you don't need to be."

"No?" She still kept her distance. "All right, I do believe I'd be safe on him so long as you told him to behave, but in the first place I couldn't get up there, and—like I told you— if I did I'd just slide off again."

"You won't slide off," he said. He got into the saddle and Halla stood still, waiting for the touch or the word that meant go.

"I'll see you both at Lammas Knowle," said Kate.

"Put your foot in the stirrup and give me your hand."

"It would be different if I'd ever been on a horse before in my life," she protested. "Even if I don't slip off I'll be shaken to pieces. What are you trying to do to me? Deliver me back to the house as a nervous wreck?"

He was laughing, not at her, with her, and she laughed too, glowing with excitement and a wonderful feeling that something fantastic and fabulous was happening. She did what she was told and there she was, perched up behind him, high off the ground. "Wouldn't I have been safer in front?" She looked down and shuddered. "Back here you mightn't notice if I go."

"I'll notice. You hang on," he said.

She clutched him, and said blithely with exaggerated calm, "Ah well, it makes a change."

"I'm sure it does." He was grinning wickedly, deliberately misunderstanding her. "You're not a clinging girl, are you?"

"You know darn well I'm referring to the transport, and it's all right to make a joke of it, but I could fall off, so you'll go slowly, won't you?" His skin looked cold, wet with rain but glowing. If he had bent his head a fraction he could have kissed her on the lips, and she turned her own face away. "Please go slowly," she pleaded.

"We'll go at your pace," he promised. He meant Halla would, of course, and then he turned and all she could see of him were broad shoulders and the back of his head.

When Halla moved off it felt like an earthquake. Although the horse was ambling, not even trotting, Kate was jolting up and down like a sack of potatoes. Her movements seemed to have no relation to Connor's. He sat comfortably, easily, and she literally bounced all the time, her teeth chattering unless she kept her jaw painfully clenched.

It was still raining, but she didn't get the brunt of that because she was hunched behind Connor, and he sheltered her. All the same, it was as uncomfortable a journey as any she had ever made, and after what seemed about an hour but wasn't anywhere near that, she gasped, "Please stop!"

Connor reined Halla to a halt and she loosed her clutch on him and put her hands in front of her face. "You'll have to put me down," she said, her voice muffled. "I'm not a born horsewoman, this is about all I can take for the first lesson."

Connor was out of the saddle, reaching to lift her down, and Kate slithered limply to the ground. "Besides," she said with horror, "I think I'm going to be seasick."

All that jolting had produced an attack of nausea, but as soon as she stood still her heaving stomach settled back into place. She grimaced, pale but recovering, "I told you you'd do better to let me walk," she said.

"The first lesson's over." The way he held her now was supporting and comforting, and the way he looked at her. "We'll walk from here."

"Thank you," she said groggily, "that's an offer I won't refuse," and she remembered Connor saying she was a girl who would always get a better offer than a man who might be helpless . . . "but not from me" . . .

She wished she had thought before she spoke. It embarrassed her for the moment, but not for long. Just as no one had antagonised her so savagely as Connor Lammas it seemed now that there was complete empathy between them. She was relaxed now, where she had always been on the defensive or the attack, feeling she could trust him as though he was her closest friend, tested a hundred times. It was all very strange, the way everything had suddenly changed.

Some of the way back to Lammas Knowle Connor led Halla, some of the way he rode at an easy walking pace, and Kate's wellbeing and high spirits returned in full measure. They talked, about nothing much, but Connor made her laugh as often as she made him laugh. She had to be tired, and of course she was, but she felt so light of heart that she could have danced in her gumboots, back over the rough grasses and through the tangling dragging undergrowth.

Once Connor suggested, "If you'd like to try riding again I'll walk by you and keep him steady," but Kate declined emphatically.

"Thank you very much, one lesson was more than enough."

He smiled. "Don't you think I've anything more to teach you?" and she laughed back,

"I didn't say that, I shouldn't think that." Connor wasn't talking about Halla, and although the wind blew cool her blood warmed and her heartbeats quickened.

When they did get back to the house they must have been spotted from a distance, because Andrew had been wheeled out and was under the archway leading into the courtyard. Gail had wheeled him and was standing beside him, and Kate said, "I have been a long time, haven't I?" and ran on ahead, over the bridge across the stream. Connor followed, leading Halla.

"What happened to you?" Andrew called. "Where have you been?"

"I walked a long way." Kate reached him. "I lost count of time."

"Do you know what time it is?"

"No."

Connor came up and said, "Don't stand there talking. Get inside and get a hot bath and a hot drink."

He took Halla past them, across the courtyard, towards the stables. Gail wheeled Andrew, and Andrew and the two girls went into the house. "Where did Connor find you?" Andrew was asking.

"Over the hills somewhere," said Kate. "He tried to give me a lift back, but I couldn't get the hang of it, so I walked."

"Connor came with you?"

"Yes." She must have sounded happy, or perhaps she smiled, because Andrew said,

"You don't sound as though that was any hardship for you. All of a sudden you seem to be getting on famously with Connor."

Kate said quietly, "Do I?" The last thing in the world she wanted was Andrew adding her to his list of reasons for being jealous of Connor. She said, "Perhaps he's getting used to me. Do you mind if I go and have that hot bath? I am rather damp."

She went to her room, depositing gumboots on the way when she realised she was leaving muddy tracks. She would have to wash her hair too, she looked like an orphan of the

121

storm. She turned on the bath taps and began to undress, and when there was a knock on her door she sighed as she slipped into her bathrobe and went to see who was there.

It was Jennifer Lammas. Over the sound of running water she said, "You are all right, aren't you?"

Kate reassured her, "I just walked farther than I should have done. After I've had a bath I'll be fine."

"Connor was worried." His mother sounded surprised about that. "He asked where you were, and when you'd gone." Her smile became smug. "He's beginning to look on you as one of the family, think of you as a sister." She patted Kate's arm in its towelling bathrobe, as though Kate was a good girl and everything was working out nicely.

Kate went back to her bath and slid into the warm silky water and let herself float away for a few minutes. This was how she had felt when Connor held her, floating and supported, warm and relaxed.

Mrs. Lammas thought Connor thought of Kate as a sister, but he didn't. He knew there was no chance of that. She was right for Andrew in no way at all, nor was Andrew right for her. Whereas Connor—

She finished her bath in a hurry, then washed her hair and briskly began to towel it dry. Connor was attracted to her—he had made no secret of that this afternoon. Superficially of course, casually, but he liked her and she liked him. After the start their relationship had had it was incredible that she should now be liking him enough to want him for a friend.

She couldn't compete with most of his friends and she wouldn't try. She had made a fool of herself on Halla this afternoon, and most of the girls Connor dated probably rode beautifully, so what did Kate have? She hoped she could paint. She wasn't bad looking, men did find her attractive, so she would just do the best she could and see what happened.

122

She put on a pink linen dress that matched the pink flush in her cheeks, and tried to cool down her cheeks with tonic lotion and an extra dab of moisturising foundation. She was usually pale and perfect-skinned, needing no more than moisturiser, eye make-up and lipstick, but she wished now that she used face powder or at least a tinted foundation. She didn't look cool at all, she looked vulnerable and troubled.

She had never felt this way before. Even getting ready for dates with men who said they were in love with her she had always known where her limits were set. But tonight she was no longer sure of anything, except that Connor Lammas was an experienced man of the world, with confidence, skill and power, and she was a long way out of her usual league.

Gail had stayed for dinner. As soon as everyone was seated round the table she announced that she had persuaded Andrew to come over to her home tomorrow, staying overnight. Andrew grinned, "She kept on nagging me, she's a dreadful nagger," and Mrs. Lammas said,

"That's a wonderful idea." She glanced at Kate. "Kate will be away until Sunday too, so I think that's a very good idea. Don't you, Connor?"

"Yes," said Connor.

Throughout the meal Kate's six-mile walk was catching up on her. She was tired and she found herself drifting into little daydreams. As usual Gail and Mrs. Lammas did most of the talking, but sometimes it seemed to Kate that there was only herself and Connor at this table. His eyes were on her all the time, whenever she looked at him. And when she looked at him, even when he didn't smile at her, it seemed as though he was smiling.

After the meal Connor left them, as he usually did after dinner, and Kate sat in the drawing room trying to keep upright in her chair and pretend she was watching television, until she had to ask if she might go to bed. She was yawning by now, and she said goodnights all round, and went to her room, expecting to fall asleep the moment her head touched the pillow.

Instead she tossed and turned. Her body was weary, but her mind wouldn't rest, and after a while she sat up in bed and began sketching. She drew Connor again. Not a caricature this time, but as good a likeness as she could. When she finished she propped up the sketch pad on the bedside table, turned off the light and opened the curtains, so that when her eyes became accustomed to the dark there was enough light streaming through the window for her to make out the features of the portrait.

She lay on her pillow, her face turned towards the sketch, mooning like a lovesick girl. When that description came into her mind she smiled at herself, because it wasn't true. But she looked at the sketch she had made, and remembered how safe and sweet it was in Connor's arms, and drifted into sleep, and dreamed she was very close to him, here in the darkness.

Moira's knock on the door with the morning tea woke Kate next morning, and galvanised her into action. She shot up, grabbed and shut the sketch pad, and then called, "Come in," and Moira got the impression that Kate was very wide awake and had something on her mind.

That would most likely be because Mr. Andrew was off to the Goweries today. Everyone knew that Miss Gowerie was Mrs. Lammas's real choice for a daughter-in-law, although she had been nice enough to Kate since the accident. Kate was popular with the staff of Lammas Knowle now, even Mrs. Shale said it was hard to tell her from a born lady. That was a compliment from Mrs. Shale, she was always impressed by 'born ladies'.

Secretly Moira thought that Mr. Andrew wasn't good enough for Kate Howard, but it would be a crying shame if Kate was elbowed out now because Miss Gowerie's father had all that money, as if the Lammases didn't have enough of their own.

Moira put down the tea tray looking so upset that Kate wanted to know, "What is it?"

"N—nothing," Moira stammered, but Kate persisted gently,

"There *is* something the matter. Can't you tell me?"

"It's not me," Moira sighed, "it's you. Mr. Andrew and Miss Gowerie."

"Oh, that," said Kate lightly. "That's all right."

"You don't want to be too sure," Moira warned her. "The mistress always had a soft spot for her, she always wanted Mr. Andrew to marry her."

"I know," said Kate.

"You do?" But Moira couldn't believe Kate knew all of it, or she wouldn't be so cheerful. "Mrs. Lammas'll get him back with Miss Gowerie if she can, on account of the master not being the marrying kind," said Moira. "All her eggs are in one basket, you could say."

Kate bit her lip on a smile, Moira sounded so earnest, and asked, "Isn't he? Connor?" This was the third time she had been told that Connor wasn't for marrying, it seemed to be something else she and Connor had in common.

"He's not looking for a wife," Moira said. "And why should he when half the girls he meets are after him?"

She knew that the master had disapproved of Kate, but he had gone out in the storm yesterday, looking for her, and over dinner Moira had seen them smile at each other, so they must be on better terms now. For the first time, in front of Kate, Moira admitted hero-worship. "He's smashing, isn't he?" she said.

"Connor?" said Kate.

"Mmm."

"All the charm in the world." Kate quoted Gail, and Moira sighed and left Kate with her morning tea.

As Moira had said, half the girls Connor met were probably amenable to advances. He was rich, and compellingly attractive, but if Kate kept her sense of humour and, of course, her head, there was no reason why this shouldn't be a very pleasant relationship. It would be exciting to have a friendly flirtation with a man like Connor Lammas.

She packed her small case for her weekend at the flat, and put in the sketchbook with the portrait she had made last night. She was taking canvas and easel and paints along too.

When she got downstairs to the breakfast room both Mrs. Lammas and Connor were at the table. Connor got up as Kate came into the room, as though he had been waiting for her. "Have a good weekend," he said. He put a hand lightly on her shoulder, pausing for a moment as he passed her, and just as she had once tried to strike him, her fingers rising instinctively, it almost happened again. Her fingers moved, but this time she caught them back, and she had not wanted to strike out. She had wanted to cover his hand, to hold his touch against her shoulder.

"Come and have some breakfast, dear," said Jennifer Lammas, and Kate went to the table and sat down, her fingers gripped together.

In friendship Kate was outgoing, generous and warm, but more than once she had had the accusation of 'frigid' hurled at her by frustrated would-be lovers. She had even wondered if they were right. But Connor's touch just now had stirred her so that her hand had reached for him as instinctively as her heart beat faster.

She was not herself, and Jennifer Lammas poured out coffee and put it before her and felt sorry for her, although she had no suspicion of the real reason why Kate was very quiet this morning.

Yesterday Jennifer Lammas had decided that Connor was beginning to accept Kate, and it had seemed that everything was working out smoothly for Kate and Andrew. But if there was a chance that Andrew might be turning to Gail again that, in his mother's opinion, would be better for Andrew because Gail was perfect for him. He and she had the same friends and the same interests, the families had always known each other; Gail's mother was one of Jennifer Lammas's oldest friends.

Kate was a dear girl, but she was very independent. And talented. She might even become a well-known artist, and then she might think her work was as important as Andrew's. Gail had no particular talents, so she would make Andrew exactly the kind of wife he needed.

Jennifer Lammas was feeling guilty as she breakfasted with Kate because, although she liked Kate very much, the hope was stirring in her that it was going to be Andrew and Gail after all . . .

Jack the chauffeur helped Kate with her luggage when she arrived back at the flat. She only had her overnight case, but the painting equipment was cumbersome and he carried it into the house, to the top of the stairs to the flat for her. She opened the door and called, "Are you two decent down there? Can I let a gentleman in?"

Janice and Susan both bounded out of the kitchenette, fully dressed, and looked up at Kate, who smiled back at Jack, "It's all right, you don't need to close your eyes."

"Just my luck!" sighed Jack. He and Elsa, his wife, would be sorry when Kate left Lammas Knowle, but they couldn't see her being allowed to marry Andrew. Now, as Jack followed Kate down the steps, carrying the easel and canvas, Janice laughed.

"Has Connor Lammas chucked you out, then?"

"Not yet," said Kate.

Jack put down his burden and said, "See you tomorrow night, ladies, about seven."

"So, tell us about it," Susan urged as soon as Jack had

gone. "You're painting? You're painting Andrew?"

"I've finished the portrait," Kate said, "and Connor said Felix Klopper will consider anything else I do for the galleries. If he does accept any of my work it would be on merit. If he turns it down, well, I won't have lost much, will I? So would you mind if I painted you two?"

She had a feverish urge to get down on canvas what this flat had meant to her, with the two girls who had been like sisters to her, and before they knew what was happening they were posed; Susan by the window that looked out on to the tiny yard, Janice at the table with the morning mail and a newspaper, both girls with coffee mugs, a typical Saturday morning scene.

While Kate roughed out her picture she gave them her news. Physically Andrew hadn't shown much improvement, but he was off with Gail this weekend and Kate saw that as a move in the right direction.

"Gail Gowerie is Andrew's steady," she explained, "but he goes off the rails occasionally and makes rather a fool of himself. It seems I was his third disaster." She told them about the other two, and like Gail they were unsympathetic at Andrew Lammas's hard luck in love.

They grinned in very heartless fashion. "No wonder his mother wondered about you," said Susan.

"And his brother tried to pay you off," Janice quipped.

"Connor actually apologised to me," Kate told them. Both girls waited.

"And?" Janice prompted, and when Kate looked blank, "Oh, come on, what made him change his mind?"

Kate smiled, remembering. "He said I was very independent and I could probably make my own way, so why should I be after a rich husband?" She added lightly, "Maybe I should have said sorry myself, because I was wrong about him in some ways."

Her two models were motionless now, hanging on her

words. "He's got a sense of humour," she admitted, "and charm. When we stopped fighting he became quite bearable."

"Fanciable?" Janice suggested, and Kate laughed.

"Bearable, I said, but I suppose if he set out to be he could be fanciable." She sounded flippant, but Susan and Janice were intrigued to hear her agreeing that she was attracted to the man she had loathed last weekend. They would have been even more enthralled if they had known that Kate had met the first man she might find impossible to resist.

"We do have the shopping to do," Janice said, an hour or so later. They had talked and talked—not about Connor Lammas, Kate had said no more about him—and Susan had more or less kept her pose at the window, Janice hers at the table. But they couldn't stay put for the whole of the morning, and Kate laid down her palette and said,

"I've made a start, I'll come into town with you. I want to tell Angus I'm taking his advice and aiming for the Klopper Galleries."

The girls caught the bus into the centre of Moorton Fells and, while Janice and Susan went round the food supermarket for their week's supplies, Kate strolled into L and L, up the staff stairs to the roof and the studio. Her three colleagues were there. Angus and Jimmy greeted her warmly, but Ken was quieter.

They asked about Andrew and she told them how he was, emphasising, though, that he would be walking again, it was just a matter of time.

"Thought you'd have been Mrs. Andrew Lammas by now," said Ken. His beard was slightly thicker than when Kate saw him last, but it was never going to amount to much and she felt he would do better to settle for being clean-shaven.

"Sorry to disappoint you," she said lightly.

"When's the wedding going to be?" Ken was getting a scowl from Angus, but Kate laughed and said,

"I'll give you all plenty of warning so that you can collect for a wedding present." Then she began to tell them about her painting. She had been joking about marrying Andrew Lammas, but she was serious about getting down to work, and Angus and Jimmy were as pleased as though she was their protégée.

Angus chuckled, "I told you, lassie, you've got the talent, we're going to be proud of you yet."

She laughed again then. "And you've got the blarney!" But she hoped that her talent would be strong enough to produce something worthwhile, that would interest Felix Klopper, and please Jimmy and Angus and herself. And Connor. She very much wanted Connor's approval.

She spent an enjoyable weekend on her 'Saturday morning' picture of the flat and the girls, and went on working until the last minute on Sunday while she waited for the arrival of Jack to take her back to Lammas Knowle.

When the doorbell rang she went to answer it. Her case was packed, she was ready. She just had to get the paint off her hands, and get into her coat. She didn't mind going back this time. She was almost eager to be going, stealing glances at the clock from late afternoon, although she was enjoying herself.

At seven o'clock exactly the front door bell rang, and that was the time she was expecting Jack. She hurried up the steps, down the hall, and opened the door, and there was Connor. Delight at the sight of him sent pins and needles through her like a slight electric shock. She gasped, "This is a surprise!" and he said,

"Is it?" and then sharply, "What have you done to yourself?"

He had looked down at her hand as she held it towards him, and seen a scarlet smear across the palm. He took it

130

gently and when she said, "It's only paint," he grinned, but he said,

"That's a relief," as though a cut on her hand would have mattered to him. Then he asked, "Are you ready?"

"Yes." She hesitated briefly. "Will you—come and tell me what you think of my painting?" She wasn't sure whether it was going to be good or not, but Connor would know. Although even if she wasn't much good she would still go on painting.

The last time he had walked down these steps into the flat he had told her she must come to Lammas Knowle and they had almost come to blows. He must be remembering that. He had seemed the most loathsomely arrogant man she had ever met, and now she was delighted to see him. This was a pretty drastic change of attitude, for both of them.

She led the way again and Janice and Susan sat up very straight with expressions of stunned surprise. They had guessed who he was before Kate introduced him, and they were so impressed that even Janice could only squeak, "How do you do?" and smile twitchily as Kate led the way to the easel.

Kate looked anxiously at Connor, and began to hedge against criticism by explaining that this was only a beginning, a lot more work had to be done yet. He turned from his survey of the canvas to her troubled face and said, "It's going to be good."

"Honestly? You really think so?"

He thought that she was capturing the warmth and home-liness of the untidy room, and her fondness for Susan and Janice showed so that anyone looking at this painting when it was finished would see friendship here. He thought it was skilful and touching, and he smiled and asked, "Would I lie to you?"

"No," she said slowly, "I don't believe you would."

Kate carried the painting out to the car, placing it on the

131

back seat. Connor carried her easel and case, Janice the palette and paints. The girls stood on the pavement waving goodbye, and as Kate sailed away in Connor's car Janice said, "There goes *the* Mr. Lammas all right!"

Susan was a thoughtful judge of character. They watched the car to the end of the road and she summed up Connor Lammas. "Andrew might not always get what he wants, but I'm sure Connor does." She was anxious for her friend. "Kate can look after herself, can't she? Kate's been around?"

"Of *course*." Janice was trying to reassure both of them. "Right from the time we were at school I don't think I've ever known a more level-headed girl than Kate."

But this was a Kate Janice and Susan hadn't known. She looked at Connor's hard profile, and he met her eyes for a moment with a flicker of a smile before his gaze went back to the road. "Hello," he said.

"Hello," said Kate.

Nothing else was said for a while, as though they didn't have to talk because being together was enough. That was how Kate felt, her head nearly but not quite against his shoulder, his hand changing gears almost brushing her hand.

They were driving through town, along streets of shuttered shops, when Connor asked, "Did you spend all weekend painting?"

"Most of it. I went into Publicity yesterday morning." The great store of L and L dwarfed the other shops around as they reached the centre of Moorland Fells. Kate had looked at all these windows yesterday, but she looked again as the car sped by. "I was asked if I was Mrs. Andrew Lammas yet," she told Connor, smiling.

"What did you say to that?"

"Sorry to disappoint you."

He sounded amused. "Who was disappointed?"

"Ken Reeves." She was about to explain, 'He works in Publicity,' when Connor said,

132

"Ah yes," as though he knew all about Ken.

"What does 'Ah yes' mean?"

"I recall the name."

He must have hundreds of employees, new ones coming, old ones leaving. "Do you know the name of everyone who works for you?" she asked.

"Not every one."

"What do you know about Ken?" She could only study him in profile and his was not an expressive face. It would tell nothing he wished to keep to himself, but he said bluntly,

"He figured in your report," and she gasped.

"How?"

"As the one before Andrew," said Connor coolly.

"The one *what*?" Ken was not even a particularly close friend, and when Connor didn't reply Kate said, "Unless they had it down as a very platonic affair your spies slipped up there."

"Did they indeed?"

"Indeed they did." She had been indignant that anyone should dare to investigate her, but now it didn't matter, although she asked, "What else was in that report?"

"Nothing that mattered," said Connor, speaking her thoughts. He looked down at her again, with the fleeting smile that softened the hard face, and she murmured,

"I'm sure you've packed more into your past than I have."

"Very likely," he said drily, "I've had more time than you."

More time, more lovers. Kate's closest relationships had stopped short of committal, but how many lovers had Connor had without considering himself committed? She looked at his hands on the wheel, and felt their touch as vividly as though she was in his arms, and wondered if she could bear to listen to the story of his life.

Mrs. Shale had a message for Kate when she arrived at Lammas Knowle. Would Kate please phone Andrew at the

Goweries'? When she did he said, "Some friends have just turned up here and Gail's badgering me to stay tonight—would you mind?"

"Of course I wouldn't mind," said Kate warmly. "I'm glad you're enjoying yourself."

"Did you enjoy yourself?" Andrew inquired, and she told him she had, that she was painting her flatmates' portraits. "If you go on like this," he said, "you'll soon have enough for an exhibition." He didn't sound too pleased about that, as though it was a real possibility and he didn't altogether approve. "You'll spend the evening with my mother, I suppose?" he said.

"I suppose so," said Kate.

But Mrs. Lammas was not at home either, she had also gone out to friends, so Kate sat down alone at the dinner table with Connor.

It wasn't too large a table, in the dining room the family used when they were alone, or the company was like Kate or Gail. But for all that it was beautiful, oval Regency, set out perfectly, the meal deliciously prepared, everything that Connor took for granted. But Kate, fresh from her weekend in the flat, found the contrast very marked.

Connor Lammas expected the best, he was born to it, he worked for it, but Kate suspected he could make himself at home anywhere. So long as he was in charge, of course, he wouldn't expect to take second place, but he was a most interesting and accomplished companion.

Kate had never enjoyed a dinner date more, if you could call this a date. There were no soft lights or sweet music, but there was a growing intimacy between the girl and the man who sat facing each other, lingering over their food, tasting wine and words slowly.

Kate was in a new element for her. It wasn't the affluence of this place, Connor Lammas's possessions, that attracted her. It was the man himself, his enormous intelligence, his humour. His physical appeal. He certainly had that. Kate had never had a crush as a child. As a woman she had never imagined herself in love, beyond a warmer affection for one man than another. But now with Connor she felt happiness opening like a rose, filling her with a sensuous delight as though the talking was lovemaking.

She told him what she had been doing with her life since her parents died. He knew the framework from the investigation report, but she filled in the amusing bits. She hadn't settled anywhere for long, but she had always made friends and worked for her living. She had been busy and thought she was happy enough. She said, "Then I ended where I started, in Moorton Fells, and here I am."

"I'm glad about that."

Meeting his suddenly serious look she said huskily, "There's nowhere else I'd rather be." If she had ever said that before she had never meant it literally till now. Against all the fascinating places in the world she would choose this room with this man.

He said, "There are places I'd like to take you," and that sounded as natural as though they had been travelling together for years.

"Tell me about them," she said, and listened while he talked about the wide world.

Moira was serving the meal, and as she gathered up dishes from the sweet course Kate noticed a stiffness in her movements, an awkward positioning of her hands. There was a ring on her engagement finger that she was trying to show to Kate, and probably had been for ages. Kate pointed, "Moira—?" and Moira beamed broadly.

Now it had been noted she could make an open display of it, turning her hand to catch the light. "Yesterday," she said proudly.

"You got engaged to Peter?" cried Kate. Peter was the only man whose ring Moira would be likely to be wearing or offered, and because Moira had been wanting to marry him for some time Kate said, "Congratulations."

"Thank you," said Moira, and when Connor added his good wishes she blushed and thanked him too.

"Who's the lucky man?" he asked, and Moira said dreamily,

"Peter Woodloe of Boddington Farm," savouring what would be her new name and address.

"We shall be sorry to lose you," said Connor.

"We're not getting married till next year, sir." Moira looked almost pretty, blushing and smiling. "I owe some of it to you, miss," she said, and Kate opened her eyes wide. "You did my hair for me," Moira reminded her. "It made Peter sort of sit up and notice me."

Kate hastily disclaimed credit, admiring the sapphire cluster and wishing Moira lots of happiness, and Moira went off holding the tray so she could watch her ring as she carried the tray out of the room. Then Kate said wryly, "I hope he appreciates her other qualities besides the way she's fixing her hair now."

Connor laughed. "The hairstyle is an improvement. I didn't realise you were responsible."

"I washed it and set it for her one afternoon, and took it out of that elastic band. It didn't take much imagination, but she did say Peter liked it. I'm sure he'd have proposed in any case, and Moira's been wanting to marry him ever since they met at the Young Farmers' Ball the year before last."

"Well, well, quite the romance." Connor stroked his long lean chin.

"I hope so." Kate spoke in low tones, the light had gone from her dark eyes, they were full of shadows now. Connor's eyes were piercing clear as he watched her, and asked her,

"You don't believe in happy endings?"

136

She tried hard to smile. "Moira will make a good farmer's wife, and he sounds a nice man. She talks about him a lot. It should be a good marriage."

"Some are," said Connor. He probably had nothing against the institution of marriage, except for himself, but Kate's attitude was based on bitter memories.

"Of course," she said.

"But not your parents' marriage?" said Connor.

No one else knew that. Not even neighbours. Not even girls and boys who had grown up with Kate. Only Connor knew, from half a dozen words she had spoken yesterday that could almost have been in jest.

There was no joking now. She didn't look at him. She sat, with elbows on the table, hands pressed flat and hard against her cheeks, and a fall of dark hair shielding face and eyes. She said, "I can only remember them agreeing once, about anything, and that was that I shouldn't go on to art school. That I should take the job in the corner shop. They hated each other, I think. They blamed each other for everything. And me. They blamed me."

"Why should they blame you?" he asked quietly.

She lifted her head and shook her hair out of her eyes. "They got married because of me. They were very respectable, I was their one lapse, and because of that they married and blamed each other until they died."

She looked at him, almost as though she was challenging him to blame her too. "That is my experience of marriage," she said tautly, "so now you see why I'm not too thrilled that I might have been matchmaker for Moira."

"They deserve to be damned," he said. He meant her parents, and she cried instinctively,

"*No!*" She stammered, trying to explain, "They were unhappy, that's what made them cruel. They might have been different apart. I don't know. They led a dreadful life together, but it's over now. Even the house has gone. The

137

whole road's gone."

She hadn't been to look. She had been told, but she could never make herself go back to look. "I've done a lot of living since then," she said unsteadily.

Living but not loving, and recalling those early years had raised barriers for her again. She was more than attracted to Connor, she found his magnetism almost overwhelming, and until a few minutes ago she hadn't had a care in the world. She hadn't wanted Andrew or Mrs. Lammas home. After dinner she had wanted to go on talking with Connor, walk in the garden perhaps, down to the lake. Or sit in the drawing room and listen to music. If he had touched her in love she would have gone into his arms because that was what she had wanted.

But now the rightness of everything was flawed. She was no longer sure. The only really certain thing about life was that people hurt each other, and she knew that Connor Lammas was ruthless and could be cruel.

She drew back. Still sitting at the table, facing him, she retreated in spirit into the old elusive Kate, who could never be hurt to the heart because her heart was never unguarded. Connor nodded coolly at what she had just said, and agreed that often the past was best forgotten. Then somehow they were talking about something else that was not personal at all.

When Mrs. Lammas walked into the drawing room half an hour later Kate was sketching, and laughing at Connor's account of Lammas Knowle snowed up one Christmas with a houseful of incompatible guests, ranging from a bishop to a mad jazz musician.

Kate was glad to see Mrs. Lammas. The sketch pad had been an excuse to sit away from Connor, but when the sketch was done and Kate showed it to Connor then—well, she wasn't sure what then, but she was thankful to see Mrs. Lammas.

Her relief must have shown, because when she glanced across at Connor his expression was wry and knowledgeable, and she realised with dismay that he was reading her like a book.

CHAPTER SIX

JENNIFER LAMMAS had just learned that Andrew was staying another night at the Goweries' and was trying to hide
her satisfaction. She didn't want Kate hurt, goodness knows
she never wanted anyone hurt, and it was a relief to see
Kate occupied with a sketch pad, and to hear that Kate had
started another painting while she was with her friends. If
Kate's career was well launched it might soften the blow
when she found she had no future with Andrew.

Jennifer Lammas had wondered if she should start dropping hints. Was it kind to leave Kate in her fool's paradise?
On the other hand, Andrew still seemed dependent on her,
and if his mother interfered it could upset everything.

Earlier in the day Jennifer Lammas had asked Connor
what she should do and been told, "Nothing. Leave it alone."
She always took Connor's advice, but there were times when
he could be almost callous, and she did hope this would not
be one of them.

Kate's sketch of Connor was very good, although Jennifer
Lammas couldn't understand why when Kate asked Connor,
"Do you think this is an improvement on the last?" he
should grin and say,

"A slight change of style, you're very versatile," as though
there was something amusing in the question. Knowing nothing of the Easter Island head she decided the comparison
must be with Andrew's portrait.

"Kate *is* clever," she said, admiring the sketch. "Her
parents must have been proud of her."

Kate flinched slightly, but smiled quickly. "I've only done
the odd sketch or painting up to now. Nothing much."

"They should have been very proud of her," Connor said
quietly, and his words warmed Kate against the cold memory

of a house in which praise and encouragement were never given.

His mother begged the sketch of Connor, but Kate still had the one she had made on Friday night that nobody but herself had seen, and she could produce another any time she wanted. That was one thing about an artistic flair, you could record people and places so that you could see them again whenever you needed them. Not that she would forget Connor's face if she left Lammas Knowle tomorrow and lived to be a hundred.

She had taken the sketch with her in her weekend case, and slept in her tiny bedroom with it beside her bed. Now she propped it up again on her bedside table in Lammas Knowle, and sat up in bed feeling somehow that it was company.

Tomorrow she would go on with the painting of the flat and the girls, the background from memory, the portraits in some measure from photographs she had brought back with her. She tipped the snapshots out now, on to the counterpane, and looked at them again. Then she thought about Mrs. Lammas's photograph album and all those smashing snaps of Andrew. And the pictures of Connor. And the girls with Connor.

She could almost see the photographs again when she thought about them: the faces of the girls, sometimes a frozen moment where a look or a hand on an arm suggested a relationship.

Kate had met one young woman who had come to see Andrew one day, one of the Lammas set, very much at home. She hadn't said much to Kate and Kate had vaguely disliked her, without even remembering her as a girl who had been photographed on a summer's day standing very close to Connor. But Kate could see that photograph now, and she supposed the little ache it brought was jealousy.

It *was* only a little ache, a smile or a touch could have

soothed it away. She could smile it away herself, because she had no right to possessiveness so far as Connor Lammas was concerned, and she hated and feared possessiveness. It was a selfish, destructive emotion that put bars on the windows and locks on the doors.

In her sketch Connor looked cool and cynical. So did the sketch she had made this evening, because that was how he did look. Even when he was angry he was still in control of himself. He looked dangerous when he was angry, but it would be hard to portray the hardening of the already hard mouth, the edge in the steel grey eyes. Anyhow she didn't want to remember him angry.

She put away the snapshots of the girls and said, "Goodnight," to the sketch of Connor. "Dream of me," she said. "It's only fair you should, because I shall probably dream of you." Then she switched off the light and before very long she slept.

Connor was finishing breakfast when Kate walked into the breakfast room next morning, and she decided that from now on she would get up earlier so that they could breakfast together. He always seemed to breakfast alone, but he said, "Good morning," as though he was glad to see her, and she wondered what his dreams had been. If he dreamed, or if he remembered. She remembered a little of her own dreams and, as she sat down and Moira came in with more coffee, she felt herself smiling and blushing faintly.

Connor could have no idea why that was, and he raised a quizzical eyebrow and asked, "What are you laughing at?"

"I wasn't laughing." She did then, though, her eyes dancing. He had a newspaper folded open, and she indicated it. "What's the news?"

"No laughing matter, I can tell you," he said, and she poured herself coffee, nodding as though satisfied.

"Which means everything's normal."

It felt normal, sitting here with Connor at the beginning

142

of the day. It felt right and natural, such a good beginning that the hours that followed must go well. "What will you be doing today?" he asked.

"Painting, I hope. What will you?"

"Meetings mainly. Dull necessary stuff." Kate could imagine him in the chair at board meetings, behind the desk in the central seat if the gathering was small and informal, and she thought she would like to know the men he would be with today and understand the things they would discuss. She wondered if she would ever be able to say at the end of a day, "Tell me about it."

He was getting up, saying, "If you go walking don't walk too far."

"Or I might find myself riding pillion again?" She closed her eyes and shuddered. "I wouldn't care for that."

"I quite enjoyed it."

"How disgustingly selfish!" Now she was pretending shocked reproach, and he said cheerfully,

"That's right." He looked across at her and her heart gave that queer little lurch. "I hope you'll be here when I get back," he said quietly.

"I expect I will be."

As he reached the door he said, "Goodbye." Neither moved, but something linked them across the room like a caress.

"Goodbye," she said, and when he closed the door after him she felt as though part of her went with him. Her thoughts were going to be with Connor many times during the day, wondering what he was doing now, at this particular moment. "Lord keep him safe," she whispered, so softly that she could hardly hear the words herself, but it was a prayer from the heart.

Jennifer Lammas came down to breakfast feeling a little guilty at Kate's smile, because Kate looked happy and Andrew's mother thought that was because Andrew was expected home any time.

They talked about the weather, the sky was clear and there was promise of a fine day, and then Jennifer Lammas opened her mail. She usually had letters, she was an enthusiastic correspondent, and as Kate poured out tea for her she said, "You never seem to get letters, do you, Kate? Don't you ever write to your friends? I do enjoy my letters." She was reading one that had come with Canadian stamps and postmark. "Jeanette and I went to school together," she said sentimentally. "A long time ago, I'm afraid, but we still keep in touch. It's good to have old friends."

Kate agreed. "I went to school with Janice, one of the girls I share a flat with, I'm trying to paint her right now. And I do write letters and get them, of course, but they don't come here. They go to my home address, the flat."

"You don't think of this as your home?" asked Jennifer Lammas. But it wasn't Kate's home, she was only here temporarily, and while she was wondering how she could explain that to Andrew's mother Andrew's mother said slowly, "If you don't see Lammas Knowle as your home how can you see yourself as Andrew's wife?"

It seemed that Kate did not consider herself established here, which would make things simpler but was a big surprise for Jennifer Lammas.

"Do you really see me as Andrew's wife?" Kate asked bluntly, and Jennifer Lammas stuttered,

"W—well, I—"

"I think Gail would be better for him too," said Kate, and Jennifer gulped, hearing what she had believed to be her hidden thoughts. Then her eyes filled with tears.

"You're a dear unselfish girl," she said tremulously. "You're a wonderful girl, Kate." She thought this was self-sacrifice on Kate's part, and Kate shook her head.

"I'm not wonderful at all. I'm thinking of myself quite as much as Andrew, because I don't want to marry anyone."

144

Jennifer Lammas was sorry to hear that. It used to be the men who had to be cajoled into matrimony, not the girls. Men were the only ones allowed to be free spirits, when marriage was the only solid sign of success for a woman. As a woman who had married well Jennifer Lammas still tended to believe that. Gail was more suited to Andrew than Kate, but Kate was a dear girl and of course she should be looking for a husband.

Jennifer Lammas said, "Of course you'll marry. You'll find a nice man—"

"Who's waiting for a nice girl?" Kate smiled, and Jennifer said,

"And why not?" Then a thought struck her. "Does Andrew know you don't want to marry him?"

"He should. He did know, but after the accident—"

"Yes." Jennifer Lammas considered this, looking down at the letter beside her plate as if it was a memo on the subject. But her eyes were not taking in the written word. She was remembering Andrew in hospital when she took Kate along to see him. "You can't walk out on me now, Kate," he had said. Something like that. His mother couldn't recall his exact words, but from what she could remember it could have been a kind of blackmail.

"I did feel some responsibility for the accident," Kate admitted. "He was showing me that he could ride Connor's horse."

"He was being very silly," admitted his mother. "But until he's walking again we shall have to go on spoiling him, shan't we?" Her voice was anxious, Kate's presence still seemed necessary to Andrew, and when Kate nodded Jennifer Lammas asked, "What will you do afterwards? When Andrew's walking again."

"And getting married to Gail?" Kate said mischievously, and Jennifer Lammas said,

"Well—perhaps—"

"Go back to the flat," said Kate. "Go back to work, and carry on painting in my spare time." Go out with her friends again and, she hoped, continue to see Connor. No, she didn't just hope, she knew that she would meet Connor again and again. Once she had wondered if there was anywhere she could hide away from him. Now there was no one she would rather open a door and see, or turn a corner and find waiting for her.

"I shall miss you," said Jennifer Lammas.

"We shall be nearly neighbours." Kate smiled. "Compared to this house my home is a small shambles, but you'd be very welcome any time."

"You'll visit us, of course?" Kate had been so helpful in so many ways. She was always considerate and competent, and Jennifer Lammas was realising how fond she had become of this girl who wasn't going to marry Andrew.

She wondered if she might suggest some time that Kate stayed on as her companion. She could do her painting, and more or less what she was doing now, except of course that she wouldn't be spending time with Andrew.

But when they were married Andrew and Gail would probably live at Lammas Knowle, and Andrew had been infatuated with Kate, and she was an attractive girl, and the more Jennifer thought about it the more imprudent her plan of Kate as companion became. She would have to accept it. As soon as Andrew was walking again, or became as dependent on Gail as he now was on Kate, Kate would be leaving here. She sighed deeply. She was pleased about Gail and Andrew, but she would miss Kate.

After breakfast Kate worked in the library on her painting. She hadn't painted alone in here before, Andrew had been her model, but now she worked in solitude, seeing the flat in her mind's eye, looking at the snapshots of the girls from time to time and seeing them too.

She was so absorbed in what she was doing that she didn't

146

hear the almost silent running of Andrew's wheelchair, nor Gail's footsteps, until Gail said, "Hi!" and they were both behind her.

Andrew looked well, and Gail looked bright and pretty, but it took Kate a moment or two to drag herself out of the image world of her canvas, and focus on the flesh-and-blood pair. They were staring at the canvas and Gail was murmuring, "Ye—es."

"If you go on at this rate you'll swamp the market," Andrew said tartly. He wouldn't be cheering if her paintings sold, Kate realised, and she asked,

"Recognise them?"

"Are they supposed to be the girls you shared the flat with?"

"You cheated," she said gaily. "You looked at the photographs," and Gail giggled, and as Kate put down her brushes and palette and turned her back on the canvas Andrew was conciliated and ready to tell her who had turned up at the Goweries'. Not that Kate knew them, but it seemed that Andrew had enjoyed himself.

He kept Kate running attendance for the rest of the day, but while he was with the physiotherapist she slipped back to her painting and Gail joined her.

"I think it's terrific," said Gail, and Kate's cheeks pinked with pleasure.

"Thank you."

"Andrew doesn't like competition." Gail sat on the table edge, swinging a leg. "That's why he's grumpy about your painting. He'd like it better if you weren't any good at it."

"Oh," said Kate. She was concentrating on Susan, who looked a little like Gail, except that Gail was a rich man's daughter from shining hair to Italian shoes. Susan was sentimental but sensible, and so was Gail. As Kate's brush followed the curve of Susan's cheek Gail said,

"Connor has always been the biggest competition in And-

147

rew's life."

"So I imagine," said Kate.

"But he doesn't have to bother about competing now." Although that was obvious Gail gave it a deeper meaning, and when Kate's eyes met hers she said slowly, "Not so long as he stays in that wheelchair."

Gail had grown up with Andrew, and still loved him, Kate was sure. She was the girl who knew him best, but for all that Kate's voice cracked with surprise. "You mean—he doesn't *want* to walk again?"

"Part of him does, of course," Gail said soberly, sadly. "But deep down he's been fighting Connor for years, losing every time, and now he can't fight, can he? He's got to be carried now."

Andrew had gone almost hysterical when Kate and Nurse Phillips had urged him to make more of an effort. Kate could imagine how he'd react to what Gail was saying.

"Have you discussed this with Andrew?" she asked, and Gail's mouth went down at the corners.

"What good would that do? He wouldn't believe it. He'd never agree he could be doing any of this to himself. It would set him back months if I even hinted at it." And Gail's relationship with Andrew could be set back for ever. "Anyhow," said Gail, "it's only a theory, I could be quite wrong."

While he was a cripple no one would blame Andrew any more if he couldn't keep up with Connor. It was a theory that made sense.

"If you're right," said Kate, "what's going to happen?"

"I don't know." Gail was still sitting on the table edge. She got off and walked a little way down the long book-lined room, nibbling on the coral varnish of a thumbnail. "Perhaps the exercises and the massage will cure him, or he might get so bored in that chair that his subconscious will let him go." Her cheerfulness had a hollow ring, and when

Kate began,

"Does Connor think—" she grabbed Kate's arm, almost sending a daub of paint across Susan's face.

"Oh, *don't* repeat any of this to Connor, please," she pleaded. "Andrew would never forgive us. Just forget I said it."

"All right," Kate promised, which was nonsense. Of course she couldn't forget, and Gail could well be right . . .

The days slid by, into weeks, into another month. Kate spent a lot of time with Andrew, as much as Gail did because Andrew was still loath to let Kate out of his sight. Some days there seemed to be a faint improvement in Andrew's condition, but the progress was never sustained. The next day there would be no response at all and Andrew would be sunk in gloom. They spent those days encouraging him, assuring him he would walk again, and although he and Gail were now as inseparable as they had ever been he still insisted on Kate being around.

Kate was content to be around, to be staying at Lammas Knowle. She had finished her painting of the flat and started on a landscape of the moors, sitting with her easel on the lawns in front of the house and painting a purple and lilac vista of distant hills. She escaped to the summerhouse on the islet when she needed to be alone, although she took Connor with her in her thoughts so vividly that if she closed her eyes it was like a physical presence.

She had breakfast with him almost every day now. No one remarked on that, she simply got up half an hour earlier and they had breakfast together. That started the day right for Kate. Just exchanging a few words, sitting watching the lean clever face, feeling the touch of his hands although he didn't touch her, set Kate up for the day. It sustained her, like food and drink. After breakfast with Connor she could deal with whatever life had in store for the rest of the day.

Sometimes they ended the day alone too. Several times when visitors had left, Mrs. Lammas had gone to her room and Andrew was in bed, Connor and Kate were still talking until well past midnight. Her liking and respect for him grew. So, she hoped, did his liking for her.

That night, when Andrew had been at Gail's and Mrs. Lammas had returned after dinner, she had thought he had wanted to make love to her. But he hadn't. Nor since. He hadn't even tried, and yet it seemed to Kate that the current of attraction between them grew stronger all the time. It certainly did for Kate. She did a lot of dreaming, by day as well as night.

Weekends she went back to the flat and if he was at home Connor collected her. This fascinated the girls, especially as Kate only smiled when Janice ventured a warning, "You're aiming a bit high, aren't you? Do you think he'll still call here after you've left Lammas Knowle?"

Kate thought he would. She smiled and shrugged and said, "Who knows?"

"Just don't get swept off your feet." Janice had never expected to be giving Kate this kind of advice, but Connor Lammas could have swept any girl off her feet. Speaking for herself, if she had been in Kate's place, Janice wouldn't have listened to warnings and she didn't expect Kate to, and when Kate said,

"Don't worry, I'm quite safe," Janice burst into rueful laughter.

"You can't believe it," she said.

But Kate did believe it. Connor Lammas was the most dangerously attractive man she had ever met, and yet she felt safer with him than she had ever felt with any other man or woman in all her life. She didn't try to explain the feeling. She knew she was in an explosive situation, there was nothing secure about it, it was dynamite, and yet when Connor was near she felt safe . . .

150

Kate had been at Lammas Knowle nearly eight weeks when Jennifer Lammas celebrated her fifty-sixth birthday. If it hadn't been for her sons, she said gaily, she would still have been celebrating her thirty-ninth. Every year she had had a party on her birthday. She loved company, but since Andrew's accident there had been no formal entertaining at Lammas Knowle.

The birthday party was planned on a smaller scale than usual and Kate would have kept out of it if she could, but Andrew wouldn't hear of that, of course Kate must come to the party, and his mother agreed with him. If Kate was absent everyone would jump to conclusions too soon, and Kate could be relied on to do nothing to upstage Gail. She assured Kate,

"But of course I want you at my birthday party."

"Very well," said Kate. "Thank you."

"What will you wear, dear?" Jennifer Lammas asked her later.

"I haven't thought about it," Kate thought, and came up with the last dress she had bought. "My green one, maybe? You remember that, you were with me when I got it."

"Of course. It's very pretty." And very inexpensive, not too much competition for Gail. "You wear your green dress," said Jennifer Lammas.

Kate hadn't worn the green dress since the day she bought it, when there had been that 'fashion display' for Andrew, and Andrew's mother had made her wear the emeralds. As she got into the dress again now Kate smiled, remembering her flare-up with Connor. The last of the flare-ups. The next day he had admitted she was no fortune-hunter, and miraculously the hostility had ended.

Or *was* it the last of the flare-ups? She walked her bedroom, brushing her hair until it crackled. She could go up in flames over Connor, be left in ashes, and knowing that she should surely be scared to death instead of smiling as she

151

looked at herself in the mirror. A tall girl in a green dress that left her arms and her white throat bare, with a cloud of dark hair swirling as she tossed her head. How could she be scared when she had dreamed a hundred times of Connor loving her, when being loved by him would be coming into her kingdom?

She went on smiling, with softly parted lips, her dark eyes languorous, as she put down the hairbrush and turned away from the mirror. Guests would be arriving in the next half hour and Kate was expected downstairs in the drawing room, where Gail was with Andrew and had probably been joined by Mrs. Lammas and possibly Connor.

She went through the picture gallery. She knew all the paintings in here now, Connor had told her the history of them all. He had bought most of the modern paintings himself, for pleasure and for investment, and when she had half a dozen pictures to show a man called Felix Klopper would tell her if she was an artist.

Connor wasn't in the drawing room. He was looking down into the great hall, leaning on the balustrade, and he heard her coming and turned towards her, waiting for her. He looked arrogant and elegant as always, in one of those superbly cut suits, pewter grey this time, with grey and white striped shirt, grey silk tie, grey silk handkerchief just showing in the breast pocket. His tie had probably cost more than her whole outfit, shoes included, and when she reached him she said, "My dress isn't bad, is it, for the Reductions rail?"

"It's a bargain," he agreed.

"Oh dear, does it really look like a bargain?" She didn't care if it did and neither, she was sure, did Connor. He took her hand and his touch beat in her brain.

"You look enchanting," he said, "but there is just one thing, your hair." It might have looked more elegant styled, it fell smoothly in a slight wave, but it suited her and she hadn't expected him to criticise her appearance. She raised her eyes inquiringly to his. "I'd suggest the Moira style," he said.

"The *what*?"

"Tied back with a piece of string."

He was joking and she grinned, glad that he wasn't finding fault. "Moira preferred an elastic band," she said. "Do you really think that would suit me?"

"If you tied your hair back it might make it easier for me to keep my hands off you." He was smiling as he trailed a hand down her arm and she felt her skin prickle. "There's something very seductive about your hair," said Connor. "It's soft and shining, and it smells very clean as though you've just come in from the rain, and I want to run my fingers through it, and that could be misinterpreted."

Anyone looking up from the great hall, or coming into the gallery, could have seen them smiling and talking and thought nothing of it. But if he had been stroking her hair that would have started gossip and Kate said lightly, "That could cause talk."

Connor shrugged, "Let them talk. It's your reaction I'm concerned with." She wanted him to stroke her hair. She wanted his hands to slide down her body, his mouth to crush her mouth, and it surprised her that he didn't know that. He probably did, with all his experience. The nearness of him turned her to a melting sweetness, soft and drowsy. He was hard, his eyes, the chiselled strength of his face. Taller and stronger and master of all he surveyed. Except for her, and he wanted her, so why wasn't she afraid?

She looked down at Mrs. Shale hurrying across the hall with a tray of glasses. The buffet was ready, everything was ready. Without looking at Connor she said, "Do I carry a 'Hands Off' notice?"

"No," he said quietly, "a 'Handle With Care' notice."

That could be tenderness, or it could be the waiting game. There would be nothing clumsy or impetuous about this man as a lover. He would handle a woman with care and with consummate skill, choosing the right time and place— and that wouldn't be in full view of Mrs. Shale if she should chance to look up.

But as Kate lifted her head he bent his head and kissed her lips, and as she gasped he smiled, "Don't worry, we're practically alone," and she had to smile too.

"I feel as if I'm in a spotlight." It was too early for electric lights yet, a warm sun-dappled evening with light streaming through all the windows, and a busy household revolving around.

She would relive that kiss tonight when all the guests had gone, and perhaps it would add up to nothing, but it had left her dizzy. "I feel like Juliet on the balcony," she said.

"Well, I'm too old for Romeo," he was still smiling, "so would you mind if I walked down rather than climbed down the chandelier?"

"Oh, please do." She did a dowager drawl. "Swinging from them is so hard on the chandeliers, and they're not easy to replace these days."

They began to walk down the great staircase together. "You didn't buy a necklace to go with that dress," said Connor.

"I didn't get round to it. Did you really think I had designs on the emeralds? My, how you glared at me!"

He chuckled, "My, how you glared back!"

"Did you, though?" It was something to laugh at now, but he said drily,

"That wasn't the thought uppermost in my mind when I walked into that room and saw you."

She had been standing in front of the Louis Quinze mirror and he had scowled at her from the doorway, as grim and forbidding as though he had caught her sneaking the jewels out of the safe. He had looked angry and sounded angry, demanding, "Don't you think it's a little premature to be decking her out in the family heirlooms?"

"Then what was your uppermost thought?" she asked, and when he said,

"How beautiful you were," she almost misjudged a step. She recovered her footing at once, drawing back. He had moved quickly in front of her as she stumbled, and she clutched the dark carved handrail looking down at him.

"Thank you," she said shakily. "That's a lovely compliment, even if it isn't true." He stayed where he was, on the stair below, turning to face her.

"It was true," he said.

"But—you were angry."

"I was shaken. From the first time I heard your name you'd been a damned nuisance, and after I met you you'd gone from strength to strength." Kate's eyes were level with Connor's. His were gleaming with wry humour. "When you tried to slap my face, you remember—?" She nodded. "I've never raised a hand to a woman, as the saying goes, in my life," said Connor, "but I near as hell hit you then."

Down below people were coming into the great hall. The birthday party was starting. Kate could see them, and Connor could hear them, but he took no notice. "I'm glad you resisted the temptation," said Kate. "You must pack quite a punch."

"I do." He stroked his chin. "And so would you have done if I'd let you."

"Could be," she agreed. "At the time my heart was very much in it."

Jennifer Lammas was greeting her first guests, wondering vaguely what Kate and Connor were talking about on the staircase and why they didn't come down. "So it was a shock," said Connor, "to realise that the woman who filled me with such uncivilised antagonism was so beautiful she could stop me in my tracks."

He looked at Kate, to the exclusion of everything. She couldn't hear the other voices now. She could only see Connor, hear what he had just said and herself stammering, "B—but I'm not b—beautiful."

"You most certainly are," he said, firmly, settling the matter. Then he looked down into the hall and the other voices rose again. "We'd better get down there." She hung back and he turned again. "Come on."

"I'd rather keep in the background," she pleaded, "and sneak down on my own."

"You'll do no such thing." He sounded impatient and she went down with him, protesting, lowering her voice as they neared the birthday guests until, by the bottom stair, she was muttering out of the corner of her mouth.

"I don't want to make a show of myself. I want Gail to be the girl with Andrew. I think I'll slip through the guests and get behind the buffet. I used to work in an hotel once, I'm a dab hand with a loaded tray."

"The Crown, Polbryn, Cornwall," Connor intoned gravely. "They gave you an excellent reference."

"That was obliging of them," said Kate. It was all in the dossier, of course; some time she would ask if she could see that report on her past. She stood still at the bottom of the staircase, while Connor was drawn away by his mother and surrounded by her guests.

The painting of Andrew, now hanging in the music salon, was generally admired, but Kate did manage to keep in the background. She sat beside Nurse Phillips, and watched the celebration of Jennifer Lammas's birthday without making any move to join in. The last party she had attended here had been that dinner party, when she had been making mental note of everybody and everything to tell the girls when she got back home. She had been hating Connor then. Hate was hardly too strong a word for the animosity that

156

had been between them, and now she was loving him, and that wasn't too strong a word either.

It was used lightly these days, but Kate had never used it before. "I love you, Connor Lammas," she said silently, to the tall figure that stood out among the milling guests. "And I should like to pour a tin of black paint over the beautiful red hair of that woman who has her clutching hand on your arm."

Catrina Hornby had been the girl at that first dinner party who never took her eyes off Connor; tonight she followed him wherever he went, until he left the party, alone and early. He came to where Kate sat with Nurse Phillips, and said goodnight. "Work, I'm afraid," he said, and Kate smiled coolly at Catrina, who was looking her way for the first time this evening, and only now because Connor was over here.

The party looked like going on till morning; it was a Saturday evening and several of the guests were staying overnight. Andrew's only sign of disability was that he didn't move from his chair. He looked very debonair and dandyish in his plum-coloured velvet suit, and gratified at the fussing of the folk around him. He didn't need Kate at this party, and no one but Nurse Phillips noticed when she slipped away.

It was some time between half ten and eleven, too late to do much but go upstairs to her room and bed. But she was restless, stiff from sitting still for nearly three hours. Nurse Phillips had been quite satisfied with the role of spectator, but Kate had grown bored with it, and was glad to get out of that chair and stretch her legs and walk around.

The night was warm and there was moonlight, and she walked out into the gardens, enjoying the effect of the different shapes of lighted windows in the magnificent old house that made it look like a backcloth for some old tale of mystery and romance.

If this had been a younger generation party there would have been others strolling under the moonlight, but Jennifer Lammas's guests were indoors, and Kate walked down to the lake's edge, looking up at the waterfall shining in the moonlight, and at the rippling mirror of the lake.

There was her island, in this fairytale setting, a place she preferred to the grandest room in the house. All her life she had escaped to the islands of her mind when the going was grim, but this was the first real solid island, no fantasy, earth underfoot, and a summerhouse of cool hard stone.

No one ever seemed to use the summerhouse. Maybe they never had and it was built as a folly to set off the island. Or perhaps it was used in quieter days when ladies sat and sewed on sunny afternoons and took tea, picnic fashion, with their friends and children. Perhaps lovers had used it as a trysting spot, perhaps a girl had once slipped out of the house as Kate had just done and run through the shadows, long skirts rustling around her ankles, to meet the man who waited for her.

That was a pleasant thought. This was a night for ghostly lovers, just the right sort of shadows, and the waterfall and the lake and the breeze in the trees made sounds that could have been laughter or softly murmuring voices. She walked over the narrow ironwork bridge, wondering about those other women who had stepped on these swaying rungs. She had never come here at night before, and it was fantastically beautiful with the black and silver water all around and the lights of the house glimpsed through the trees.

If there were ghosts she hoped they wouldn't mind her intrusion, and she smiled at her fancies, and pushed open the door of the arbour, and almost screamed. A tall shadowy man stood by the window, but before the scream was out she had recognised Connor and her breath escaped in a long feeling sigh as she sagged in relief. "Oh, you scared me! I never dreamed anyone was in here. I was thinking about ghosts."

"Sorry about that," he said, "but ghosts don't usually smoke cigars." She could smell the familiar aroma now and see the glowing tip of the cigar he held. "What brought you?" he asked.

"I've had enough of the party. I was taking a walk before I went to bed. I often come here in the afternoons, I didn't know anyone else ever did, I thought it was my secret island."

"So did I." She could just make out his expression and she could hear the smile in his deep voice.

"Do you come here often?" She wasn't being flippant, although that sounded as though she was, and she added quickly, "I mean, I've never seen you here. Although I wouldn't, would I, because I always come in the afternoons and you're never around during the day, except at weekends when I'm—"

"I should have known," he said, across the nervous babble of her voice. He was still standing by the narrow window, almost blocking it, outlined by moonlight.

"How could you have known?"

"Your perfume." Kate's perfume varied, she bought whatever took her fancy and was within her price range at the time, but it was possible that even an inexpensive scent could linger for a few hours in this small closed room. If Kate had been here during the afternoon and Connor had smoked a cigar in here at night.

"And I should have known," she said. Cigar smoke and aftershave, the sensation of his presence when she was alone here, dreaming. "I thought I imagined it," she said.

"So did I." He must have been thinking of her. She must have been in his head as he was in hers. "Are you coming in?" he asked.

Perhaps she looked poised for escape in the doorway, but

159

her only escape was where he was, that was where she was safe. He made no move until she took a step towards him, then he held out his arms and she took three more paces and they were locked together, fused in a passion that took her breath, her only reeling thought that if he loosed her she would die.

She had to hold him, locking her fingers at the back of his neck, crushed against him, needing his mouth on hers as though he would breathe life into her.

He saved her, kept her alive with a kiss. Later she would realise that was all it was—a kiss. Deeply different from the brief light pressure of that earlier kiss this evening, but it was not a claim nor a promise. It was a man who knew almost all there was to know about lovemaking. Kissing a girl who, despite her modern looks and outlook, was virginal and, until she had met him, unawakened.

She had to know that, but every nerve in her body was clamorous with desire, and she would have responded, sweetly and instinctively, to whatever way of loving he had shown her.

He showed her gentleness, his lips brushing her hair, her temples, his arms around her no longer crushing but cherishing as though she was precious and fragile. "You amaze me," he said huskily. "You fill me with wonder."

Kate was filled with wonder herself, bemused and bewildered. "No one comes here," he said, "except the gardeners to cut the grass. No one but me. Now it seems I've been waiting for you all these years."

Her islands had been lonely places, but on this one love had waited. She trembled and he said, "You're cold."

"No." The night was warm and she had never been cold in here, although she remembered Andrew's description. "Andrew said no one used this place because it was cold and damp as a ditch. But it isn't cold."

"And that was why you came here, to be alone?"

"Yes."

When he asked, "Will you share it with me?" she laughed softly.

"If you'll share it with me."

"I'll give it to you," he said. "You'd make an enchanting Lady of the Lake."

Kate could almost believe she was an enchantress, who could hold a lover for all eternity. Connor had two long furrows across his forehead, a deep line between the brows, and she ran a fingertip along them as though she could smooth away the problems that made him frown, and teased, "But are there conditions to being the Lady of the Lake? Would the lady have to settle for the lake for ever, and never leave it?"

"A prisoner on the island? That wouldn't do for you, would it?" She loved his voice, deep and slow with laughter in it. "How about a part-time Lady of the Lake?" he asked.

"That I think I could manage."

"I'm sure you could." He sat down on the circular seat that ran round the wall and drew her down beside him, and she curled comfortably with his arm around her, her feet tucked up, her head against his shoulder. Smoke rose lazily from the discarded cigar on the ground and she said lazily,

"You wasted a good cigar there."

He laughed. "I couldn't risk setting fire to your hair."

"Very considerate." She sniffed appreciatively. "And I've no complaints, it still smells as expensive smouldering away on its own, but wouldn't you like to light up another one?"

After a moment he said drily, "I see what you mean." She had had no ulterior motive, and she couldn't think of one until he took his arm from around her, and a cigar case from his pocket. A match flared briefly, and she realised he thought she was calling a halt to lovemaking. Maybe she had been, without realising it, afraid of the unknown.

He wasn't annoyed. He smiled at her, and with the cigar

alight put an arm around her again and asked, "How was the party when you left it?"

"Swinging." She amended that, her head back against his shoulder. "Well, going at a steady respectable pace. Andrew seemed to be enjoying himself."

"Good."

She could lift her head and see his face, or stay as she was and settle for jawline and cheek. She said, "He and Gail will marry, won't they?"

"They may."

"I hope they do."

"I thought you were against marriage."

"It isn't for me." She was used now to the faint echoing of voices in here, but those words seemed to go out into a great distance, a lonely frightening sound, and she said quickly, "Marriage wouldn't do for me, but for Gail and Andrew I think it might. Don't you?"

"I'm no fortune-teller," said Connor cynically, and Kate sighed.

"Maybe I should be getting back," she said, and Connor didn't try to dissuade her. He stood up, helping her to her feet, and they came out of the arbour, walking over the springy grass of the little islet to the bridge across the lake.

Lights were still on all over the house, and as Kate went ahead over the bridge, looking down at the dark water, she heard herself say, "Catrina Hornby was looking very glamorous tonight," although goodness knows she didn't want to talk about Catrina in the least.

"She usually does," said Connor, behind her.

"Is she—a particular friend of yours?" Kate sounded slightly amused—well, that was how she was trying to sound.

"Yes," said Connor. Once across the bridge he walked beside her, heading for the archway into the courtyard, towards doors at the side and back of the house rather than the main entrance into the great hall; and Kate found herself wondering if that was because Connor didn't want to rejoin the party. Or if, perhaps, he didn't want to walk in on the guests, out of the night, with Kate.

"She looked as though she had a claim," said Kate.

"Up to a point," said Connor quietly. Of course she knew there had been other women in Connor's life, there still could be, but it seemed he counted himself committed to nobody. No one could lay entire claim to him, not even particular friends.

From the turf underfoot to cobblestones, from comparative brightness to the shadows of the archway, with the tall dark man walking beside her and jealousy piercing her.

Were you lovers? she wondered. Are you still lovers, but does loving mean no more to you than the desire of the moment? Do you think perhaps that I shall love lightly and easily, causing no trouble?

But Kate could not love lightly. Connor was the first man she had ever wanted, in body and brain and spirit. That was how she needed to share. All of him for all of her. He thought she was sophisticated and experienced, but in the ways of loving between a man and a woman she was neither, and somehow she had to tell him that he was the first. Then he would understand that for her this was not casual nor passing, that if he said, "I love you," it must mean more than, "I desire you."

As they came out of the archway into the empty courtyard she said, "Would you care to hear about my lovers?" There had to be some curiosity, they were surely close enough for that.

"It won't take long," she was going to say, "because I never had a lover. Men have told me they loved me, I don't know whether they did or not, but I've never been in love and I've never taken a lover. Not Ken. Not Andrew. Not anyone."

But he didn't even check his pace, and the smile he gave

her was ironic. "I think not," he said. "As you once reminded me, I've probably packed more into my past than you have, so let's leave it at that. There's no need to particularise."

She blushed from head to foot, scalded with shame. Did he think she was being provocative, trying to make him jealous after his admission that Catrina Hornby had been more than a friend? Or, worse and likelier, had he no interest in the men she had known before him because his interest in Kate was strictly here and now, no past and no future?

He opened a door for her and she passed him, going into the house. She was suddenly weary, her temples throbbing. She pushed back her hair, and her face was still hot with the burning blush. She felt it warm against her fingertips. "Goodnight," she said, "and thank you for the island."

He smiled as though she amused him, and that hurt, because although she was smiling too there was no laughter in her. She said brightly, "I'll see you in the morning. Look for me in the crowd."

Catrina was one of the guests who were staying the night. "Goodnight," said Connor, and Kate went quickly, up a side staircase to her room.

She was too confused to be sensible. She couldn't think at all, she could only feel, remembering that kiss and how she had clung to him and how wonderfully right it had been in his arms. He had held other women, but the past didn't matter. It was tonight that mattered, and she was shaking so badly she could hardly open the drawer where she kept the sketch of Connor that stood on her bedside table each night.

She hadn't used that sketch pad again. It backed the sketch so that she could just prop it up, as she did now, then she crumpled on the bed, so near tears that she had to blink to see. "Don't go to Catrina," she whispered. "Please don't go to anyone, because I don't think I could bear it."

Sardonic and cynical, that was how she had sketched him, because that was how he was. But as she sat there, blinking damp eyelashes, she began to think. If Connor was having an affair with anyone here tonight he wouldn't have been alone in the summerhouse. He went there to get away from people, just as Kate did. To be alone. He hadn't minded Kate's coming. "It seems I've been waiting for you," he'd said, but he hadn't been waiting for Catrina, and as the agony of jealousy receded it was replaced by a growing conviction that she would trust him. With Catrina. With any woman.

He had not asked her to trust him, nor told her that she could, but she was comforted. Getting undressed and ready for bed she smiled at the joke they shared, that he had given her the island. She was still smiling when she fell asleep ...

She was up early next morning, but Connor was earlier. He had gone riding; and Kate went walking, because Mrs. Shale told her that the only one up yet was the master and he'd gone off on that brute of a horse of his. And when Kate wandered out to the stables the groom told her that Connor had gone riding alone.

She wanted to meet him on the moors again. He had found her before, miles from the house, and she had a crazy hunch that he would ride that way again and know that she would come. After last night, and the island, it seemed almost as though he had said, "I'll ride out and wait for you."

It was a fine morning and as she climbed the hills and walked through the bracken she was almost sure that any minute she would see Halla ahead of her on the skyline. She looked into the distance so that a couple of times she didn't notice what was beneath her feet until she went sprawling.

Once turning her foot on a grass hummock, another time when the ground shelved suddenly.

Last time Connor had found her, sheltering from the storm, half way up a hill. She went in that direction, but she had better not walk that far this morning—especially as she had told no one she was wandering off—and after the best part of an hour she began to retrace her steps back to Lammas Knowle.

There was no storm today, there was lovely summer sunshine all around, but she hadn't found Connor, so although the sun shone, she felt bleak and lonely. The exercise hadn't hurt her, but so much for her hunches.

Three women were strolling on the lawns in front of the house. One was Catrina, who spotted Kate, crossing the main track, and pointed her out to the others. They all looked hard at Kate, as she came over the bridge over the stream, and that was odd as well as embarrassing because they had all seen her last night, and she couldn't think why she had suddenly become worth staring at.

When she reached them Catrina asked, "*Where* have you been?" as though Kate had been reported missing with a general alarm out, and Kate said,

"I've been for a walk. What's the matter?"

"A friend of yours has arrived," said a tall languid lady, looking pained.

"Who?" asked Kate, and the two older women made similar gestures, shrugging, shaking their heads, tight-lipped. They didn't know names, but they disapproved all the same.

Catrina said promptly, "He has a snake tattooed on his arm. He might be quite dishy if you like them rough, and it seems you do—he says you used to live together."

Kate remembered the tattooed snake. It writhed in her mind as she recalled the man who went with it. Tod Mulden was a none too savoury specimen. He was the main reason

166

her stay in that artists' commune in Wales had been so brief.

Catrina gave a throaty chuckle at Kate's gasp of dismay. "Hard luck," she said maliciously. "Has your colourful past caught up with you?"

CHAPTER SEVEN

KATE could well imagine the effect Tod Mulden would have on Jennifer Lammas and her guests, especially if they misunderstood what Tod had said about him and Kate 'living together'. Kate was no snob. None of her friends was rich or famous, but she would have welcomed any of them any time, without considering for a moment that she should apologise for them. But Tod Mulden was no friend of hers. She would have opened the door very reluctantly to him and the sooner he was on his way the better.

Anyhow, what did he want with her? she wondered. Annie, one of the girls who had lived in the commune, had the address of the flat. Tod could have traced her through that, although she couldn't see Sue or Janice directing him to Lammas Knowle.

In the courtyard was a motorbike that was very likely Tod's, and as Kate walked down the passage from the courtyard Mrs. Shale came out of the kitchen, unsmiling. "Your friend's having something to eat," she said, as though she begrudged the food.

Tod was sitting at the kitchen table, with the remains of a meal in front of him: cold meat and pickles, bread and cheese. Elsa was washing up, and Mrs. Shale went back to the dresser and putting knives and forks on a tray. Both women seemed to be stationed where they could watch Tod while keeping as far from him as possible.

It was nearly two years since Kate had seen him, but in appearance he had hardly changed. A hulking young man in his mid-twenties, coarsely good-looking, with dark wavy greasy hair, tight denims, a faded blue short-sleeved shirt, the snake tattoo on his arm, and the ingratiating grin of the born scrounger. There was a black leather jacket slung over the back of the chair and a grubby kitbag standing beside it.

"Hello, Kate girl," said Tod effusively.

Kate moved closer to the table and Tod's voice dropped to conspirator level. "What's the set-up, then?"

"How did you find me?" Kate was speaking very quietly too. She didn't want any of this broadcast, although the whispering was probably giving Mrs. Shale and Elsa a wrong impression.

"You write to Annie," Tod mouthed back. "I called at your address and an old girl told me you were living here." Mrs. Harris from the ground floor flat, probably. "I thought you were working here," he added. "I came out on the bike and asked a couple of old biddies where I could find you." He speared a pickle onion on a fork and crunched it like a toffee apple. "One of 'em asked me if I was 'a friend of Miss Howard's.'" He did a passable take-off of a plummy accent and grinned. "I told 'em yes, we used to live together." Kate glared. "Bit of a giggle?" he suggested. "You should have seen their faces!"

"They didn't think it was funny," snapped Kate, and Tod sighed, shaking his head.

"No sense of humour? Pity."

This was a permissive age, but Kate could visualise the fastidious shudders that bit of misinformation would evoke. It gave her the shudders herself. Mrs. Shale went out of the kitchen, giving them a disdainful look in passing and getting a wolf whistle from Tod in return.

"So—what is the set-up?" Tod whispered again at Kate.

Elsa had had the taps on and been swishing water around the sink. Suddenly the taps were silent and the water gurgling quietly away. "There is no set-up," Kate hissed back. "I'm just staying for a while."

"Doing what?" Tod's voice was getting hoarse, and when Elsa left the kitchen too he took a swig of tea and reverted to normal pitch. "That's better. What *are* you doing here?"

"Helping to nurse one of the family," said Kate.

"I didn't know you were a nurse." Tod looked and sounded suspicious. "I thought you were a painter."

"Well, I'm both here, and when you've finished eating you'd better be on your way."

He sat back in the chair, waving the empty fork at her admonishingly. "That isn't very friendly."

"I never was very friendly," she said crisply. "Remember?"

A pass from Tod had speeded her out of that commune. "You're my kind of woman," he'd told her, and she had told him—not in a million years. It had shaken Tod, until then he had thought he was irresistible.

He sighed and shook his head at her now. "That's right—you weren't, were you? Thought yourself a cut above the rest."

No, she had not, but she was in no way Tod's kind of woman. "So—goodbye," she said.

"All right, all right." He rubbed his fingertips together. "How are you for the ready? Any going spare?"

She was receiving the same salary she had earned in Publicity, but she still paid her share of the rent of the flat and her savings were small. She wasn't being bullied into handing them over to Tod Mulden. She still hoped to buy that small car some day. "Why should I give you money?" she demanded.

"Ah, come on," he cajoled. "They're calling you Miss Howard—none of your Kates. You've got to be sitting pretty here. They've got to think something of you, and you can soon tell them how it was about the living together. All we shared was the roof."

His grin looked suddenly wolfish. "Take it another way, though. You were never friendly, but I've got imagination. I could tell that high-and-mighty lot tales that would curl their hair."

"About *me*?" He could tell nothing about her, but he nodded, still grinning.

"About you and me."

He could lie, and they could believe him, because Kate was an unknown quantity, a girl with a past no one talked about. It would embarrass Mrs. Lammas horribly, in front of her friends, and it would be a body blow to Andrew's pride. "Poor old Andrew's done it again," they'd say. "This one could be more trouble than the other two put together. How much do you think it will cost Connor to pay this one off?"

It wouldn't cost Connor anything, but it might cost Kate more than she dared risk. What would Connor believe? And even if he suspected Tod was lying he might still decide that a girl who knew dubious characters like Tod Mulden could be more trouble than she was worth. She had to get Tod out of Lammas Knowle, and she had to make him go quietly, and that meant paying him.

"Stay here," she said.

"No rush," said Tod.

But Kate rushed. She only had a pound or two here, and she wasn't keen on handing Tod a cheque, he might try changing the amount before he cashed it. Normally she could have asked anyone in this house for money, and paid it back later, but with Tod around Gail seemed the likeliest one. She would be sympathetic, and she wouldn't expect any detailed explanations. Someone told her where to find Gail and she went running.

Five pounds should be enough, but better be on the safe side and give him ten. So long as Tod didn't discover he had the whip hand he would take ten pounds and consider he had made a killing, but if anyone told him Kate was Andrew Lammas's girl-friend then he would think he had stumbled into a goldmine.

Then she would have to tell Connor and, if he didn't

believe her, it would be degrading and dreadful, and when one of the guests tried to stop her as she hurried along the corridor she sidestepped the arresting hand.

"Sorry," she said, and fled from the would-be customer who had wanted a word about having his daughter's portrait painted.

Gail was with Andrew and several others, reading the Sunday papers that had just been brought out from Moorton Fells. When Kate walked into the library, where they were sitting around, everyone looked up at her murmuring greetings. It was the first they had seen of her this morning, but they all knew that Tod had been waiting for her. They went back again, rustling and turning the pages, apparently absorbed in what they were reading, but there was no chance of Kate speaking to Gail in here without being overheard, so she had to say, "Please, Gail, could you spare a moment?"

Andrew, who had avoided looking at Kate before, jerked up his head at that, and Gail said quickly, "Of course," and followed Kate out of the room. Outside she asked, "What is it?"

"I'm sorry about this." Kate was hating it. "But would you have ten pounds on you that you could lend me until I can get to the bank tomorrow?"

"Of course." Gail hesitated. "For—er—what's his name?"

"Tod Mulden," said Kate. "Yes."

Gail still hesitated, trying to put this tactfully.

"Kate, you and he—weren't—were you?"

Kate looked at her without a word, and Gail coloured. There was a fastidiousness about Kate, a reserve and a dignity that answered Gail's question and brought her to a stammering apology. "I'm sorry, that was stupid of me, but why do you want to give him ten pounds?"

"He's down on his luck," said Kate.

"I'll get it." Gail went back into the library to fetch her

handbag, and Kate took the money gratefully and promised,
"I'll give it you back tomorrow."

"No rush," said Gail. "You know that."

That was what Tod had said—no rush. He was sitting
where Kate had left him. Moira was in the kitchen now,
and Tod appeared to be chatting her up. She was looking
hot and bothered, and he bade her an ogling goodbye as he
got up and ambled out with Kate. In the corridor he said,
"Got it?"

"Here." She thrust the two fivers at him and he eyed
them with what seemed like surprise.

"It must be some job you've got here," he said.

"I like it," said Kate. "And I don't expect to see you
again."

He stashed the money in his hip pocket, then he chuckled,
enjoying himself, and asked, "Not even at the wedding?"

She stiffened, the muscles in her neck and stomach con-
tracting painfully. "What wedding?" She tried to sound
puzzled, but he knew. He must have questioned Moira. If
he had asked anyone else they would probably have said
that Kate was a friend of the family, and been off-hand about
giving him even that much information. But Moira, caught
alone, would be flustered and embarrassed, and stammer that
Kate was here because Mr. Andrew wanted her here after
the accident.

"You've done well for yourself," Tod leered. "Annie said
you worked for Lammas and Lammas. She never mentioned
you were marrying the bossman."

The last time Kate wrote to Annie she had still been
working at the store, and anyhow there had never been any
question of her marrying Andrew. She had always known
that she would not. "Andrew Lammas," she said quietly, "is
marrying a girl called Gail Gowerie. She's here now. She's
next in line for the Gowerie supermarkets, as well as being
a knock-out, and they've been going around together since

they were kids. I promise you, there's nothing between Andrew and me."

"Yeah?" Greed was glittering in his eyes and now she knew that she should have offered him less money, much less. She had admitted how high the stakes were, and how scared she was that he might blacken her character in this house. "I'd like to meet 'em," Tod smirked.

He could have told Andrew any lies he chose. But the lies would get to Connor and she couldn't face that. She said, "That isn't possible. Just go, will you?"

There were people in the corridor, and everyone who passed stared for a moment. Her panic was showing, and Tod knew he was on to a good thing. He had looked Kate up on the off-chance of a free meal. From his brief acquaintance with Kate Howard he had expected her to be earning a fair living, she wasn't an idler, but a meal was all he had expected, and now he saw the chance of real profit. Besides, she had turned him down flat and he had fancied her. Now he was getting his own back. She had been the cool one, but now he was scaring her.

He clapped a hand on his hip pocket where the money was. "Make it fifty," he said, "and I'll go."

"I can't get any more."

"But you will get it. You won't want me coming back here?"

"*No.*" Colonel Mather, one of the guests, passed them, giving Tod a second and a third look. When he was out of earshot Tod said, "O.K. See you tomorrow in Moorton Fells. Three o'clock outside the post office. After that I'll be moving on, and good luck to you and no hard feelings."

"I'll be there," Kate croaked.

She wanted to run back into the security of the house, but she had to make sure that he went without speaking to anyone, and she walked outside with him, across to his motor-bike. He gave her a quick triumphant grin, and a hug

174

that she couldn't avoid. "Three o'clock," he said, and went roaring off over the cobblestones.

Kate stood transfixed, quaking with horror as she realised what she had done. She had let Tod blackmail her. She had paid him, and agreed to pay again, to get him out of the house, because she felt that he could make Connor despise her. It was one thing for a sophisticated man of the world to say, "I don't want to hear about the lovers in your past," especially when there were none. But it was a very different matter for a creep like Tod Mulden to claim that he belonged to Kate's past. It would be her word against Tod's, and she was trying to buy him off, and what did that look like but guilt?

Anyhow, how could she be sure he would go away tomorrow and the blackmail would stop? Of course it wouldn't, and she must have been simple-minded to imagine she could keep this from Connor. She had to tell him. She had to explain.

She had been staring, unseeing, at the archway through which Tod had just vanished in a cloud of dust, and as she turned she saw Connor, grim-faced, his mouth a straight hard line. "Who the hell was that?" he demanded curtly.

"It was—" her mouth was dry, "someone I—met once." She licked her lips and tried again. "That artists' commune—"

"Indeed?" he drawled. "Well, I'd appreciate more discrimination in who you invite to this house."

"I didn't invite him," she protested, and Colonel Mather moved forward with a discreet clearing of the throat.

"I think perhaps, my dear," said the Colonel, retired Guards, M.C. D.S.O. J.P., "that Connor's right. That young feller is a wrong 'un."

Kate agreed, and she could guess how the Colonel knew. "I recognised him just now," the Colonel was saying. "Something familiar about him, and it's just come to me. Thomas

Mulden. Sent him down for six months once for mugging. Very dicey record."

Connor's frown deepened. "How long has he been here?"

"About an hour," Kate faltered. "I—went for a walk. He was here when I got back."

Connor swore, then said,

"Thank you, Colonel, we'd better check how Mr. Mulden passed the time before Miss Howard returned to entertain him. I have a responsibility to my mother's guests, I shouldn't like him to have acquired any souvenirs of his visit."

Lammas Knowle was full of treasures. If Tod had had the chance he was capable of picking up anything that was small and valuable. Kate should have considered that, and he had a kitbag. She thought wildly—the emeralds! Could he open a safe? And she remembered the jewellery the women had worn at the party last night, and was almost ready to accept that the kitbag was stuffed with loot worth a fortune.

"Where was he when you got back?" Connor was asking her.

"In the kitchen."

He strode ahead to the kitchen, followed by the Colonel and Kate. Moira was still there, and Mrs. Shale had returned. Connor said, "There was a young man in here just now."

"There was," Mrs. Shale sniffed, and Kate knew that she was alone. Connor was furious with her, giving a jailbird the run of Lammas Knowle. He didn't want her excuses nor her explanations. He was only concerned with his property, and she said in a high clear voice,

"He has a police record. You'd better count the spoons."

Moira gasped, but Mrs. Shale looked smug. "You don't surprise me at all," she said. "And don't worry about the spoons, I kept an eye on that lad from the moment he set foot in this house. He sat there at that table until you came."

"Thank you," said Connor. "If he returns he's not to be admitted."

"He won't come back," said Kate.

"You can guarantee, can you?" His eyes were cold and his voice was curt, and she said, as coldly,

"For what my guarantee's worth."

"As you say," he said grimly, and she knew that Tod couldn't blackmail her because she didn't matter to Connor. He found her enchanting only so long as she caused no trouble. If she became tiresome she was dispensable.

She looked very self-possessed as she walked out of the kitchen. The Colonel was saying something about Mulden being a plausible chap who could easily fool anybody, and who could be going straight as a die now for all the Colonel knew.

Except for a little blackmail on the side, thought Kate wearily. And he hadn't fooled Mrs. Shale. Nor anyone. Everyone who had seen him had thought he was a discreditable chapter in Kate Howard's past.

Catrina spotted Connor and came running towards him with a squeal of delight. "Why didn't you tell me you were going out riding? I could have come with you." Without waiting for an answer she wanted to know, "Have you met the old friend who's come to look Kate up?"

"I just missed him," said Connor.

"Oh, what a shame!" Connor Lammas was uncatchable, Catrina knew, but she still went on trying, and whatever Kate Howard's role was in this household Catrina resented her proximity to Connor. "You must have mixed with some very interesting people, Kate," said Catrina. "Do many of them call on you here?"

Kate smiled brilliantly. "That was my first caller," she said, "and no doubt it will be my last. Excuse me." And she went upstairs to her own room, which wouldn't be her room much longer.

Andrew wouldn't mind her going now. This was the very thing to undermine his infatuation. Tod Mulden had done her a favour there. When all the guests had gone she would say that she would like to leave. She would apologise about Tod, although he hadn't done much harm. He had cost her ten pounds and given the visitors something to talk about. And he had shown her that Andrew hadn't been the only one suffering from illusions.

In these past weeks Connor had seemed like part of herself, under her skin, so close that she couldn't imagine how it would be if he drew away. She had thought the pain would be too terrible to endure, and she couldn't face it now. As she had done as a child she shut her mind to what was happening around her. She couldn't go to the island in the lake, but she could retreat behind the quiet barrier of her mind, thinking of tomorrow, when she would be away from here, think of the next picture she would paint.

Last night they had all said the portrait of Andrew was good, and Connor had said, "Kate's going to make a name for herself."

"How do you know that?" she'd asked, and he'd smiled at her. "I've been investing in paintings long enough to know what I'm talking about. I can tell you what Felix will say."

But she wouldn't think of Connor. She would just think of her painting and wonder if she could paint instead of living, and how she could create anything if she never dared let herself feel again.

She went downstairs at last. The number of visitors was decreasing. They were all leaving some time today, except perhaps Gail, who tried to chat to Kate as though everything was normal, and with whom Kate talked and smiled. Connor looked through her, arrogant and unreachable as at their first meeting, and she had been a fool imagining that

178

he was human, and a man she could have trusted to the death.

Catrina Hornby was one of the last to leave and, when she heard her saying goodbye to Mrs. Lammas and Andrew, Kate wondered if Connor was going with her. They left the room together, and Kate hoped he wouldn't come back for a long time because then she could say what she had to say and leave before he returned. From the other end of the long room Kate watched the door so intently and unblinkingly that her eyes began to smart.

She was almost sure he wasn't coming back when he did, and her heart leaped, because now the ordeal ahead would be worse. That had to be the reason she had to bite her lip so hard. It couldn't be because, no matter how fiercely she fought for self-control, the unexpected sight of him would always make her heart leap.

He was nothing to her. Well, perhaps there was a physical attraction, but that would soon fade if she never saw him again, and when she left here she would be out of the Lammas Knowle set for ever.

Good riddance to them all, she thought, although she had once believed she could combine the two worlds well enough, keeping her old friends and making new. But that was when she had thought that Connor loved her.

She had thought that. As she looked down the drawing room, and knew that the moment was here when she was going to say a fairly bitter goodbye, she knew she had believed that he would stand by her, through anything, because he loved her.

She walked alone down the room, past the chair where Connor was sitting, to Jennifer Lammas, and said quietly, "I owe you an apology. I'm sorry an acquaintance of mine gatecrashed the party."

Jennifer Lammas's smile was forgiving. "I'm sure you couldn't help it, Kate," but Andrew spoke up.

"Was that all he was, an acquaintance?"

Kate snapped, "Yes." She resented the implication, and she faced him and Mrs. Lammas and Gail. She would have faced Connor too, if she had turned her head the merest fraction, but she couldn't look at Connor while she explained about Tod.

"That artists' commune is a big old farm building, outhouses mainly, in Snowdonia, in Wales. There were about twenty young folk around when I was there. Some were drop-outs, I suppose, but most of them were working hard. They'd got the place for a song and they were restoring it into a crafts centre. It's on a tourist route and it was open to the public, and I was down there on holiday and I walked around."

She didn't have to tell him this. She didn't have to explain anything, but she went on, her voice so steady that Connor could never guess how she felt. "One of the girls suggested I should stay, and I did, for just over three weeks. I helped with the cooking, and I whitewashed a lot of walls, and I painted some landscapes."

"What did your acquaintance do?" jeered Andrew.

"Very little, I should think," said Kate. She remembered Tod helping with the whitewashing of a barn, but she hadn't taken much notice of him or what he was doing, until she had realised that he was taking altogether too much notice of her, and that was when she'd left.

"You kept in touch?" It was still Andrew, asking the questions.

"I write to Annie sometimes," she explained. "She still lives down there. Tod cleared out a long time ago, Annie said, but he must have turned up again and she must have mentioned me. Anyhow, he had the address of the flat."

"Do you know many like him?" Still Andrew. Not a word from Connor, he wasn't getting involved.

"Not many," she said stonily. "But I do know a good

many who wouldn't measure up to this." Her sweeping gesture covered the magnificent room. "In fact I can't think of one of my friends who does, and that includes me, so I'd always be an embarrassment to you, and more trouble than I was worth, and you really don't need me hanging around here any longer, and I would prefer to leave right now."

The direct challenge made Andrew look sheepish, and Jennifer Lammas's protest was impulsive and genuine. "Oh, but surely there's no need to—"

"Oh, but there is," said Kate.

"Connor," his mother appealed to him, "tell Kate there's no need for her to go dashing off like this."

"She may stay as long as she likes," said Connor coldly. "But I see no reason why she should prolong her visit if she prefers to leave."

He meant that Andrew didn't need her any more, and he, Connor, never had, except as a brief diversion. Kate clenched her hands tightly, and that meant that she could manage a polite little smile, and say coolly, "I would prefer to leave. Could someone take me right away?"

Not you, she begged silently. Please, not you.

"Jack will run you into Moorton Fells in the morning," said Connor.

"You'll keep in touch, Kate?" Jennifer Lammas's sweet face and soft voice were troubled. "You will visit us?" she pleaded, and tried to smile. "And you did invite me to your home, didn't you?"

"I invite all of you," said Kate lightly. She tossed back her dark hair, and looked at them: Gail looking sympathetic, Andrew disconcerted, Connor bored. That was how Connor looked, bored, uninterested, and no expression on a man's face could have hurt Kate more.

As she turned to go Andrew asked suddenly, as though trying to justify himself, "If this man is nothing to you why did you give him money?"

Kate shrugged slightly, and Gail said hastily, "I didn't say anything, Kate."

"She didn't need to," said Andrew. "She came back for her handbag, so what you wanted to see her about was probably money."

"There's deduction," said Kate, brittle and bright and on a razor edge of breaking up in front of them all. Except that she would die before she would break before Connor.

"What's wrong with helping somebody who's down on their luck?" Gail was demanding.

"Not a thing," Andrew sneered, and Gail jumped up and stood in front of him, glaring down, her voice rising high.

"You can't understand what being down on your luck means, can you?"

"What would you call this?" Andrew struck at his legs, but seeing him sitting in judgment on Kate had angered Gail. Kate had done all she could for him, she had been in constant attendance and never complained, and Gail had had enough of Andrew feeling sorry for himself. She was about to issue her own terms. She drew a deep breath and said shrilly, "I'd call that cowardice. You could walk, but you're scared to let yourself because then they'll be comparing you with Connor again, and you'd rather drop out, wouldn't you?"

Andrew didn't answer. He stared, as though hypnotised, and she went on before anyone else could speak, "You'll always be second to Connor because that's what you are, just as I could never paint like Kate, and you'd better believe it."

She sounded exasperated enough to shake him, like the spoiled child he was in many ways. "I suppose I'm in love with you," she sighed. "I've always thought I was. But I'm not spending the rest of my life with a drop-out, so you can make up your mind whether you're walking before the end of the week or not, because that's as long as I'm giving you!"

In the hush that followed Kate slipped away, and went upstairs to her own room again. If Gail's theory was correct the shock of facing the truth could get Andrew on his feet again. Kate hoped it would. So long as he was in that chair some of the blame was hers, although surely she had paid for the error of judgment that had brought her to Lammas Knowle that first weekend.

She had wanted to leave then, as soon as she arrived here. Instinct must have been warning her what lay ahead, but all she had to get through now was just the rest of this evening and one short night, and then she was free.

She packed, very slowly to pass the time. She tore the sketch of Connor from the sketchpad and was about to rip it to pieces before she dropped it in the wastepaper basket, but it was more contemptuous to toss it away whole. She had no use for it, but it didn't move her to anger. It didn't move her at all. It was simply waste paper.

Moira brought her some food, looking so worried that Kate tried hard to reassure her that, although she would be leaving in the morning, everything was fine and exactly how she wanted it to be.

Night fell and her watch seemed to have stopped more than once. But it ticked when she listened, so time was still dragging by. Both Gail and Mrs. Lammas looked in to say goodnight, they both seemed very hopeful about Andrew, and Kate smiled for them, saying she was very tired and she was sure they would understand, and she would see them in the morning.

She was very calm, she might have been tired, and at last she got ready for bed, bathing in leisurely fashion, slowly brushing her hair with the silver-backed brush for the very last time.

She didn't even have a headache. She felt nothing. She

183

was numb and empty, as though she was drugged for an operation where she could lose an arm or a leg and go maimed for life.

She got into bed. It was strange, no sketch of Connor on her bedside table. But she could see it in the wastepaper basket, and a quickening of pain jerked her upright. She couldn't lie down and of course she couldn't sleep. If she relaxed she might not get this mask of calm on again. She could weep all night and next morning everyone would know. Connor would know. When she faced him next morning he would see that she had wept all night.

That was when she knew she had to creep out of this house as soon as everyone else was asleep, and walk across the moors to Moorton Fells. Slowly, slowly the time passed, until it was midnight, half past, one o'clock, and then she turned off the lights in her room and came out into the corridor.

She could hear no sound, except for the creaks and stirrings you could always hear in old houses at night, ancient timbers shifting in their sleep, ghosts treading softly. There seemed no other lights on and if she came across anyone she would say she was going to walk in the gardens. It was late, but she wasn't sleeping, they wouldn't try to stop her.

She reached a side door and unlocked and unbolted it, and then she was out into a bright moonlit night, intent only on getting away from this house as fast as she could.

It was when she stood on the bridge over the stream, and looked across at the lake in the moonlight, that she began to cry. Running and weeping. She hadn't wept since her parents died, but now she couldn't stop and it didn't matter, there was no one to hear or see her.

She would have to stop running, she couldn't run for five miles, and she could turn her ankle on this track. After a few minutes she forced herself to slow down, to choke down the sobs. It was an airless night, oppressively warm, and she unbuttoned and unbelted her trench coat. She must walk carefully. It was light, but moonlight threw deceptive shadows.

Kate rubbed the tears from her face with the back of her hand, and then she realised that she was being followed. Until that moment her distress had blotted out all other sounds, but now she heard footsteps and when she looked back she saw Connor. Tall and dark, only a shape, but it was Connor who had once said, "I can't leave even you in the middle of the moors at this time of night," and who would take her back so that Jack could drive her safely away in the morning.

She said, "I'm walking home."

"Kate . . ."

If he came closer he might see the tears on her face. As she had done before she backed from the track into the rough grasses of the heath, and, when he followed, as she had done before she ran. He could see her for miles in this white coat . . . she must have been spotted leaving the house . . . she should have worn something dark . . . if he did catch up with her whatever happened she mustn't let him see she had been crying . . .

She tripped and had no time to scramble back to her feet, and shook her hair over her face so that he couldn't see, and glared at him through the tangle when he stooped to her.

"Don't touch me!" she said. She lifted a hand as though she would have struck him, and remembered him saying, "There'd better not be another time," and she tried to hit him, to push him away, but it was hardly a blow.

When she touched his cheek he took her hand and held it, palm upwards, to his lips. "Don't go, Kate," he said huskily.

"You don't want me to go?" That was what he was saying, but she couldn't believe it, even though his, "God, *no!*" was almost a groan.

"Why didn't you say so?" He had given no sign that what she did mattered one whit to him. He had been ice cool, completely self-possessed, but now in the moonlight he looked desperate.

"Because I couldn't have kept my argument rational," he said. "If I'd started begging you to stay I'd have gone to pieces, and I didn't need an audience for that."

His calm was a mask too, a stiff-necked pride to hide his inmost thoughts, just like hers. She said, in wonder, "You're begging me to stay?"

"On my knees, it seems." He was on his knees beside her. A corner of his mouth lifted, in the self-mockery she loved, as she loved everything about him.

"About Tod—" she began, and he said quietly,

"Don't meet him today, Kate. Please."

"I don't want to see him again. I never wanted to see him."

Connor looked puzzled. "But yesterday you looked after him as though you couldn't see anyone else."

"Was that why you were angry with me?"

"I was angry with myself," he said wryly. "Jealousy is uncivilised and barbaric, but I wanted to gallop after him and ride him down. The past I don't care about, but I came out of the stables and he was holding you in his arms. I heard him say, 'Three o'clock, then,' and the colour changed in your face as you watched him go. When you saw me you flinched, and I cared about that. That hurt like hell."

Connor was jealous of *Tod*. Kate didn't know whether to laugh or cry, it was so crazy. She almost did both, shaking her head vehemently. "*No*, you couldn't have been more wrong. He'd heard Andrew was supposed to be interested in me and he said he'd tell everyone that we were lovers. That's why I borrowed the money from Gail. I had to meet him today and pay him some more."

"He was *blackmailing* you?" It was Connor with mixed feelings now, anger and incredulity and relief.

186

"I suppose so. Yes, yes, he was. And it wasn't true. I couldn't stand the man, but I was scared you might believe him."

Connor sat beside her and cupped her face in his hand, looking at her wordlessly for a moment. Then he said, "Don't you know that it wouldn't matter? That you could come to me and tell me you'd done murder and it would make no difference to the way I feel about you?"

She should have known. She should have known she could have trusted him with her life. He took a handkerchief from his pocket and wiped her face, stroking her hair gently, very tenderly, and Kate sniffed and whispered, "How did you know I was running away?"

"I saw you from the arbour. I had a faint hope you might come there tonight." He put the handkerchief back in his pocket, and with his arm around Kate they sat on the soft turf under the stars. "Yesterday morning," he said, "I rode out to the place where I found you in the storm."

Her hunch had been right, everything was right. She gasped and laughed. "But that's where I set off for, only I turned back too soon. Next time I'll go all the way."

"You do that." His arm tightened and a tremor ran through her. "There was something I wanted to discuss with you," he said. "Either there, or on the island, or failing both at breakfast tomorrow—if we got the breakfast table to ourselves."

"What?"

He sounded calm, almost amused, but his arm around her trembled, she could feel it, as he said, "It's been increasingly borne in on me in recent weeks that in everything but a legal ceremony I am married to you."

"*What*?"

"Do you know the marriage service?" The dark face was so close, one brow quirked. "For better for worse, for richer for poorer, in sickness and in health," he quoted. "And

187

something about love, comfort, honour and keep, forsaking all others. That is how I feel about you, Kate."

He slipped the trench coat from her shoulders. She was wearing a plain cotton blouse, short-sleeved, V-necked, and Connor ran light fingertips under the stuff of the blouse on the smooth skin of her shoulders. "That you are flesh of my flesh," he said huskily. "How do you feel?"

That she could not live apart from him, that she must be close to him so long as she lived. "Don't you think you could bring yourself to marry me legally, Kate?" His caress was sensual and frankly arousing, controlled but with an increasing ardour. "Will you take me for your lawful wedded husband?" he asked, and somehow she nodded.

With a sound that was almost a sob he looked into her eyes. He was smiling but there was no laughter in his eyes, and no lightness in his voice now. "I love you," he said. "That is the simple truth. You are all the loves I'll ever know and whenever you need me I'll be there. Do you believe that?" She nodded again.

"You were reared in a bad marriage," he said, "but ours will be a good one, I promise you." His mouth came down on hers, slowly, but the kiss was deep and passionate as he held her even closer. "The best of marriages," he said. "The very best."

Kate had never intended to marry, but now it seemed as natural that she and Connor should be husband and wife as that the sun would rise tomorrow and the birds would sing. They belonged together, and her thoughts were only of this strong man and how safe she felt with him, and how sure she was that their loving would last for ever.

romance is beautiful!

**and Harlequin Reader Service
is your passport to the
Heart of Harlequin**

Harlequin is the world's leading publisher of romantic fiction novels. If you enjoy the mystery and adventure of romance, then you will want to keep up to date on all of our new monthly releases—eight brand new Romances and four Harlequin Presents.

If you are interested in catching up on exciting and valuable back issues, Harlequin Reader Service offers a wide choice of best-selling novels reissued for your reading enjoyment.

If you want a truly jumbo read and a money-saving value, the Harlequin Omnibus offers three intriguing novels under one cover by one of your favorite authors.

To find out more about Harlequin, the following information will be your passport to the Heart of Harlequin.

collection editions

**Rare Vintage Romance
From Harlequin**

The Harlequin Collection editions have been chosen from our 400 through 899 series, and comprise some of our earliest and most sought-after titles. Most of the novels in this series have not been available since the original publication and are available now in beautifully redesigned covers.

When complete, these unique books will comprise the finest collection of vintage romance novels available. You will treasure reading and owning this delightful library of beautiful love stories for many years to come.

For further information, turn to the back of this book and return the INFORMATION PLEASE coupon.

the omnibus

A Great Idea! Three great romances by the same author, in one deluxe paperback volume.

A Great Value! Almost 600 pages of pure entertainment for only $1.95 per volume.

Essie Summers

Bride in Flight (#933)
...begins on the eve of Kirsty's wedding with the strange phone call that changed her life. Blindly, instinctively Kirsty ran — but even New Zealand wasn't far enough to avoid the complications that followed!

Postscript to Yesterday (#1119)
...Nicola was dirty, exasperated and a little bit frightened. She was in no shape after her amateur mechanics on the car to meet any man, let alone Forbes Westerfield. He was the man who had told her not to come.

Meet on My Ground (#1326)
...is the story of two people in love, separated by pride. Alastair Campbell had money and position — Sarah Macdonald was a girl with pride. But pride was no comfort to her at all after she'd let Alastair go!

Jean S. MacLeod

The Wolf of Heimra (#990)
...Fenella knew that in spite of her love for the island, she had no claim on Heimra yet — until an heir was born. These MacKails were so sure of themselves; they expected everything to come their way.

Summer Island (#1314)
...Cathie's return to Loch Arden was traumatic. She knew she was clinging to the past, refusing to let it go. But change was something you thought of happening in other places — never in your own beloved glen.

Slave of the Wind (#1339)
...Lesley's pleasure on homecoming and meeting the handsome stranger quickly changed to dismay when she discovered that he was Maxwell Croy — the man whose family once owned her home. And Maxwell was determined to get it back again.